"Everybody thinks you're perfect for the job,"

Josh assured her.

"Who's everybody?" Suzann demanded to know.

He counted with his fingers. "Well, there's me…and…" A mischievous grin appeared on his handsome face and he touched his second finger. "Then there's me, of course, and there's…"

"You?" She laughed softly. "I think I get the picture." Suzann shook her head. "Josh Gallagher, you're impossible."

"Impossible?"

He gazed down at her, the tender light in his sky blue eyes reminding Suzann of the brief kiss they'd just shared at her doorstep.

Her smile faded and she looked away.

"Nothing's impossible," he said quietly. "You just have to go after what you think God wants for your life."

MOLLY NOBLE BULL

A lifelong Texan, Molly Noble Bull is married and the mother of three grown sons, Bret, Burt and Bren. She and her husband, Charlie, also have three preschool grandchildren and are hoping for many more. They own a home in the Texas hill country, but currently live in Victoria, Texas.

Both her father and her maternal grandfather were ranch managers, meaning they were real-for-sure Texas cowboys, and all three of her sons are involved in cattle ranching today. Molly spent part of her childhood on a sixty-thousand-acre, south Texas cattle ranch. When she writes about cowboys like Josh Gallagher, her hero in *Brides and Blessings,* she is writing from personal experience.

Besides her writing, Molly is involved in Christian causes and is interested in Bible prophecy. She also helped form three Internet loops for Christian women who write romance novels. She encourages readers to write to her in care of Love Inspired/Steeple Hill, 300 East 42nd Street, Sixth Floor, New York, New York 10017.

Brides and Blessings
Molly Noble Bull

Love Inspired®

Published by Steeple Hill Books™

STEEPLE HILL BOOKS

Steeple
Hill™

ISBN 0-373-87054-X

BRIDES AND BLESSINGS

Copyright © 1999 by Molly Noble Bull

Printed in U.S.A.

Bless the Lord, O my soul: and all that is within me, bless His holy name.

—*Psalms* 103:1

To my three grandchildren—
Bethanny, Dillard and Hailey Bull,
and to my critique partner, Kathryn King Brocato.
But to God give the glory.

Chapter One

It was now or never.

Either Suzann Condry exchanged identities with her twin sister within the next ten minutes. Or she flew back to California and forgot the whole idea.

The morning sun streamed through the east window of the rustic living room. Suzann drummed her fingers on the arm of the tan leather couch. When her sister came up with the idea, it had seemed like the perfect solution to Suzann's problems. But actually going through with the deception produced unsettling feelings that she hadn't anticipated.

Suzann gazed at her twin sister, seated beside her. "Thank you again, Holly, for agreeing to meet me. Taking a two-week vacation from your job in order to be here couldn't have been easy to manage."

Holly's smile beamed softness and serenity. "Mother always said that at the time of my adoption, she learned that I had a twin sister somewhere. I just didn't know how to find you until you phoned me from L.A. It was icing on the cake to discover you're also famous."

"I wish I'd known about you," Suzann said, "but I didn't know a thing until I found my original birth certificate after Mom died. But I mentioned that, didn't I?" Suzann shook her head, hoping to clear her mind. "I'm more stressed than I realized."

"That makes two of us."

The plan sounded simple enough. Suzann would become Holly Harmon. Holly would become Suzann Condry—former child movie star, actress, model, national icon.

For the first time in her life, Suzann would be free of glamour, fans and glitz. A new identity, no matter how brief, would also give her a means of escaping an unhappy relationship, and the clutches of the paparazzi.

But had the past two weeks with Holly in an isolated cabin in the Texas hill country been long enough? Did she know her sister well enough to swap lives with her?

Everything happened quickly. One minute Suzann was going through her mother's things after the funeral, the next she was phoning her agent, telling him she was adopted and asking him to hire a private detective to search for her birth parents. Mike phoned a reliable detective agency the next day and signed on one of their investigators to handle the case.

Discovering that she was the daughter of an unwed, teenage mother was surprising. She practically fell out of her chair on learning that she had an identical twin sister.

Once she got Holly on the phone, the sisters set up the get-acquainted meeting at the cabin. At their first face-to-face, it was Holly who suggested that they switch lives, perhaps because Suzann had shared how depressed she'd been lately. Suzann's actor boyfriend, Greer Fraser, had dumped her for another movie actress, and her heartbreak had been smeared all over the tabloids.

At first, the mere idea of assuming her sister's identity shocked Suzann. To begin with, such a disguise would never work. Suzann's face and figure had been on movie screens, in magazines, and on television since she was in diapers.

Holly attempted to convince her sister that she would look different without that heavy makeup she constantly wore in California. When Suzann finally saw how much Holly looked like her with makeup, she was persuaded to give the madcap idea a try. Still, even at this late date, she had doubts.

Suzann squinted at the autumn-kissed hills beyond the east window. They couldn't have found a more beautiful setting for their scheme.

Holly's transformation still amazed her. Bleached-blond hair, carefully applied makeup, and a designer outfit hid her sister's true identity. But no amount of makeup could hide Holly's winsome smile or the wide-eyed innocence of her chocolate-brown eyes.

Holly peered at Suzann questioningly. "I'm doing the innocent stare thing again, aren't I?"

"Really, Holly, I think you look great. Still, you're going to have to keep working if you hope to look like Suzann Condry."

Holly bit her lower lip. "I'm trying, really."

"I know you are. You know you really are a dead ringer for me," Suzann said, hoping to encourage her sister. "In fact at the moment, you look more like me than I do."

Holly laughed nervously. "A lot has happened in two weeks, hasn't it? I think letting your hair go back to its natural color and the black-rimmed glasses add just the right touch. Now, if I can ever get used to these contacts, I guess I'll be all set."

Holly was warm and tenderhearted. She was also naive. Was Suzann expecting more of her sister than Holly could give?

Absently, Suzann curled a lock of her long, dark auburn hair around her forefinger. "Do you think we can pull this off?"

"I certainly do."

"Then I think we can too," Suzann said with feigned optimism. "You know, I've dreamed of this."

"Dreamed of what?"

"A normal life." Suzann smiled thoughtfully. "I've been in the limelight since before my second birthday. This will be my first opportunity ever to live like normal people do, and I owe it all to you."

"Think of it this way—you're giving me the chance to wear designer clothes and live in a mansion in the California hills. What more could I want?"

"How 'bout your life back?"

"I'll get it back in six months," Holly said. "That's soon enough for me. Still, I'm unsure how to play a movie star."

"At least you won't have to do any acting," Suzann said. "Playing a church librarian in Oak Valley, Texas, might be the hardest role I've ever taken on."

Holly shrugged. "The only acting I've ever done was a role in a church musical."

"You'll do fine," Suzann said. "And remember, Mike will be right there to help you out, anytime you need him." Suzann smiled. "Mike McDowell's a sweetheart. And the best agent I know. But don't let all that charm fool you. I'm paying him big bucks to show you the ropes in California."

"I'll try to remember."

Suzann wanted to kick herself for reminding her sister that she paid Mike to be nice to Holly.

"I'm sorry," Suzann said beseechingly. "I shouldn't have said that. Sometimes I can be pretty thoughtless, I guess. But I never meant to hurt your feelings."

"You haven't."

Suzann feared that she had. Something was bothering Holly.

"Tact is seldom necessary in Hollywood," Suzann explained. "In the future, I'll try to remember I'm not in Tinsel Town anymore."

"I'll try to remind myself that I'm not *me* anymore," Holly said. "I'm you now."

"And I'm you." Suzann tried to make her voice sound perky and inspiring. "Doesn't this sound exciting?"

"Yes," Holly said under her breath. "Yes, it does."

Suzann's upbeat comment hadn't lifted her sister's spirits. She wondered what would.

"You hinted that you have a secret crush on the youth director at your church. What did you say his name was?"

"Josh Gallagher." Holly laughed self-consciously. "Some of the women in my Sunday School class call him Sir Gallagher-had."

"I believe there was once a famous knight by that name."

"So I heard." A trace of a smile still lingered in Holly's eyes. "And for your information, I never said I had a crush on him. Josh doesn't know I'm alive. I said he was good-looking. Probably every single woman in the church noticed that."

"I stand corrected." Suzann wiggled her nose teasingly. "Now, back to Mike." She put her hands on her knees. "I want you to feel free to phone him at any time and for any reason."

"All right."

"He'll also be your escort whenever you go out socially, so he can tell you who is who among my circle of friends. Any problem with that?"

"Not at all. I'll need to be with someone who knows who I really am. Otherwise I would never be able to go through with this—this disguise."

Suzann's throat felt dry and sore. However, she'd learned long ago that mentioning one's aches and pains proved pointless. The show must go on—no matter what.

She reclaimed her mug from the coffee table and

blew away invisible steam before lifting it to her lips. The warm liquid soothed her burning throat.

Somehow, the sugary taste and the scent of fresh coffee also triggered still more thoughts on her physical condition. Was she sick instead of tired? Impossible. Suzann Condry was never ill.

She swallowed slowly and glanced back at her sister. Holly had already demonstrated what a kind, straightforward person she could be. Still, how could Holly possibly fit into the world Suzann had left behind? And deep down, was Holly wishing she'd never suggested that they make the switch?

Five weeks ago Suzann didn't know she had a twin sister. Now that she'd had the opportunity to know Holly, they had bonded in ways Suzann never thought possible. A lump formed in her throat. It wouldn't be easy to say goodbye.

"Holly, it's not too late to back out. Are you sure you want to go through with this?"

"I'm sure. And I have no intention of backing out."

"You can't know how much this means to me," Suzann said. "And how much I appreciate what you're doing."

"You're my sister. We're family now."

Suzann reached over and hugged her sister. "You're great."

When the sisterly embrace ended, Suzann took Holly's hand in hers and held it. After all the years of living as an only child, it felt good to have a sibling.

Yet in a few minutes, Holly and Mike would take

a limo to the airport in San Antonio and fly to California. Suzann would settle into Holly's apartment here in Texas. They wouldn't see each other again for months, and there were still so many things they had never discussed.

"Holly, what's the real reason you agreed to do this?"

Holly hesitated as if she was going over something in her mind. "I'm doing this because of you."

Suzann pressed her hand to her chest. "Me?"

Her mother's locket under her palm felt cold and as unyielding as Greer Fraser's heart. Suzann moved her hand to her face, touching her chin with her forefinger.

"You hardly know me," Suzann added.

"Don't be silly. You're my twin sister. Why, I already love you."

"Is that the only reason you're doing this?"

"Not entirely." Holly focused her full attention on Suzann. "I happen to think there's something missing in your life. Something important. Stepping into my shoes for a few months, you might find out what that important something really is."

Suzann inclined her head toward her sister, planning to ask what could be more important than a normal life. Out of the corner of her eye, she saw Mike, standing in the doorway.

"How long have you been there?" Suzann asked.

He grinned, first at Suzann and then at Holly. "Not long. And it's time to go, Sue. It's a long drive, and our plane leaves in less than two hours."

Holly didn't move a muscle.

"He means *you*, Holly," Suzann said. "You're the only Sue in this room now."

"I know he meant me. It's just that—" Holly's voice cracked with emotion "—after all these years, I've finally found my sister. I'm not ready to give her up yet."

"I'm not ready to give you up, either."

Holly and Mike left a few minutes later. Suzann stood at the window until the rented limo disappeared behind a hill.

She gathered her things and locked the cabin. Then she settled behind the wheel of Holly's compact car and flipped on the heater. At the fork in the gravel road, she turned onto a narrow, two-lane highway, speculating about what lay ahead.

She already missed Holly, and there was so much to do and so much to remember. Recalling everything Holly had told her about Oak Valley and her new life there might prove more difficult than memorizing a scene from a movie script.

Now what was the name of that good-looking assistant pastor who also served as the youth director at Holly's church? Oh, yes, Josh Gallagher. Suzann smiled to herself. After hearing Holly rave about the man for two weeks, her curiosity level had reached an all-time high.

The highway snaked around rocky hills and over numerous low-water crossings. Holly had prepared her for huge trees, clear running water, and a hint of fall colors brightening the landscape. Yet the sheer beauty of a late-October morning in the Texas hills astounded her. If she didn't know better, she would swear she was driving through the autumn countryside in Vermont or Connecticut.

Suzann had grown up in L.A. Holly had spent her growing-up years on a Texas ranch. Though their lives couldn't have been more different, some similarities were astounding.

As children, both twins hated math, loved art and music, and were poor spellers. Both sucked their thumbs until they were four years old, got the chicken pox the Christmas they were six, had big orange tabby cats as pets and liked to keep things neat and tidy.

If that were not enough, Suzann and Holly put on identical blue sweat pants and matching tops on their second morning at the cabin without knowing what the other twin planned to wear that day. Suzann still couldn't understand it all. However, Holly had suggested she read a book on twins who were separated at birth. Suzann resolved to buy a copy.

A white water tower in the distance told Suzann she would soon arrive in Oak Valley. Holly had said the town all but shuts down by noon on Saturdays. Suzann glanced at the hand-drawn map Holly had given her. A native Californian should be able to find Holly's apartment with no problem at all.

The apartment on the second floor of a mom-and-pop apartment house looked even smaller than Suzann expected. Still, a rush of excitement filled her as she opened the door for the first time.

Inside the doorway, her eyes widened, taking in the deep blue and off-white color scheme, and the quaint, antique furniture. Just what I would have chosen, she thought. And lace curtains. Perfect. She put down her suitcases. It seemed identical twins—even when separated at birth—were more alike than she had dreamed possible.

A document in a wooden frame hung over the bookcase. Suzann crossed the room for a closer look. Holly's college diploma stared at her from behind clear glass.

Her twin sister had said she was a university graduate. Now Suzann also knew that Holly graduated from Baylor with a degree in English and library science. Very impressive.

Suzann always dreamed of going to college. But how could she? As the main breadwinner in her tiny family, it was a wonder she managed to graduate from high school.

Oh, she'd taken courses in drama at an exclusive school in New York City, but that didn't count. Her studio paid for the courses, and she was pressured to take them.

Pressured should have been her middle name. Growing up, adults manipulated her constantly. Was it surprising that now, as an adult, Suzann had a problem making decisions?

Suddenly tired, she sat down and leaned back, gripping the maple arms of an aged rocker. The wood felt good under her hands, strong, like solid families. She'd never experienced that kind of closeness. She'd merely simulated that emotion when the movie script called for it.

Oh, her mother had loved her, all right, and was always just and kind. Yet for whatever reason, her adoptive mother, Nancy Condry, was distant—seldom kissing or hugging Suzann. As an adult, she still struggled to fully understand.

Her adoptive father died in a car accident less than two years after Suzann was born, and her mother had needed a means of support for herself and her baby daughter. It couldn't have been easy, rearing a child alone.

Nancy Condry stumbled into the world of baby modeling and child acting by accident. One of the few choices for a poorly educated, single mom living in California twenty years ago.

Suzann's birth parents were an even bigger mystery, and Holly hadn't been much help. However, Suzann would soon know the truth. Private detective Roger Bairn had promised to locate her birth parents and reveal all the secrets of her past.

She eyed a photo album on the lamp table beside her chair. Her sister had thought of everything. Suzann ran her hand across the smooth, leather cover, then opened to page one.

Her mirror image in pigtails, and wearing a blue-and-white gingham dress, grinned back at her. Holly was probably about ten years old and stood between her two younger brothers. Their parents smiled proudly behind them.

Now there was a *real* family. Suzann imagined two little girls in the picture instead of one. The fantasy warmed her.

A mental list of all the chores she'd proposed to do that morning interrupted her musings. I should unpack, she thought. Reluctantly, she closed the album, promising herself that she would return to it later that day.

She would be wearing Holly's clothes. The only items she needed to put away were her personal belongings.

Then she planned to trek the six-and-a-half blocks to Oak Valley Bible Church. Walking instead of driving would give her the opportunity to see Oak Valley, firsthand. The exercise wouldn't hurt, either. She recalled that Holly had said nobody but the janitor would be at the church on Saturday morning. She could explore the building without being disturbed.

The name *Josh Gallagher* flashed through her brain again. If her interest in men was as similar to Holly's as her taste in home furnishings, she would find him appealing.

Rule number one. Josh Gallagher is strictly off-limits. If this crazy idea of Holly's was going to work, she must constantly remind herself of that important guideline.

Suzann coughed and sneezed her way to the hallway leading to the church library. She would take a quick look inside, then turn around and go back to the apartment.

Just outside the door, another coughing spell paralyzed her temporarily. Her throat still hurt. She coughed again. This was *not* the time to come down with a cold.

She took a sip of water from the fountain nearby, then another. As she reached out to open the door, she thought she heard someone coming.

Suzann froze. She'd found empty buildings un-
nerving since she was a child. She pulled her hand
back from the door-knob and slipped her key ring
back in her purse.

The janitor—yes, that's who it is, she thought.
Now, what did Holly call him? Oh, yes, Turner. Al-
bert Turner.

Whirling around, her mouth formed the letter *M* for
Mister Turner. A tall, broad-shouldered man in a
white, western-style shirt, jeans and brown cowboy
boots came around the corner. Could this cowboy be
the church janitor?

"Miss Harmon." He propped his arm against the
door frame. A one-sided grin emerged. "How was
your vacation?"

"Great."

His eyes sparkled. "Then are you rested and ready
to get back to work?"

"Do I have to answer that?"

"Absolutely."

The corners of his mouth still turned up, revealing
even white teeth. His brown, wavy hair looked thick
and coarse. Yet she knew intuitively that it would be
soft to the touch.

The bronzed tan on his weather-worn face and
strong-looking hands suggested an outdoorsman.
Jeans and cowboy boots painted an even clearer picture. Everything about him told of a working man
who spent hours in the Texas sun.

But what kept her looking at him were those blue
eyes that appeared to glow with energy and excitement. Their sky-blue color contained specks of a

deeper blue and were edged in navy, giving his entire gaze an intensity that she found compelling.

"Having trouble opening the library door?" he asked.

"Yes, as a matter of fact. I've lost my key."

Not *lost* it, exactly. She just couldn't figure out which key fit without trying all of the keys on the ring. A task she'd rather perform without curious witnesses. But the excuse gave her the chance to talk to him for a minute. She suspected that he wasn't a janitor. She wanted to learn his identity before she ran into him again.

"Here," he said. "Try mine."

"Thanks."

So, he had a master key. Maybe he was the janitor after all. Or maybe he was...

Of course.

He didn't fit her idea of a man of the cloth. Yet this too-handsome cowboy had to be none other than Josh Gallagher, the youth director and assistant pastor.

After seeing him, she knew why he'd captured the notice of all the single women in the congregation. That lean muscular body and long legs left no doubt.

"Don't forget," he said, "Pastor Jones wants us to work on that duet for next Sunday."

"You don't mean tomorrow, do you?"

"Tomorrow's *this* Sunday." His engaging grin held a pinch of laughter. "Don't worry. We still have two weeks to practice. Do you have a copy of the music yet?"

"Yes. I mean— You know, I can't remember."

"Don't let it bother you. I'll run off a copy of mine."

Suzann nodded her thanks and put the key in the lock. As she reached back to return his key, another coughing spell erupted. She felt slightly light-headed and feverish now along with her other symptoms.

Without a word the cowboy reached for a paper cup above the fountain. He filled it and handed her the water.

"Here," he said, "drink this."

She put the cup to her lips and drank. The urge to cough slowly vanished. The cool water also relieved her aching throat a bit. But she still felt woozy.

"Thanks," she said. "I needed that."

"You sure did." His deep chuckle filled the air. "Are you all right?"

"I'll—" she swallowed "—I'll be fine."

"Did you know it's getting dark outside? Looks like rain."

"In that case, I'll cut my visit to the library short."

"Can I get you anything?" He hesitated thoughtfully. "We have cough drops in the church office. I'll go get you some."

"You're kind to think of that."

When he'd gone, Suzann sat down at the desk, put her head down and closed her eyes. When she finally lifted her head again, she studied the room, searching for some sort of work that she could be involved in when the cowboy returned. Turning in her chair, she pulled out a book from the bookcase behind her.

The *Church Directory*.

She'd been wanting something that would acquaint

her with the congregation at Oak Valley Bible Church. A church directory was just the text she'd been hoping to find. She would check it out of the church library and take it back to Holly's apartment for further study.

She filled out the library card and opened the book to the first page. She'd just turned to the *G*s for *Gallagher* when Josh reappeared with the cough medication. Casually, she flipped to the *R*s.

"How's the cough?" He handed her the box of candied drops.

"Better." She popped a drop in her mouth. "Yum, cherry-flavored. My favorite."

"Keep the whole box then. We have several cartons of the stuff in the church office."

"Thanks again."

He shifted his weight from one long leg to the other as if there was something more he wanted to say. "As you know," he began, "I'm new to Oak Valley, and I thought the pastor said you were a native Texan. But you sure didn't sound like it just then."

She needed to forget her cough and get in character.

"I have several friends from other states." Suzann's sculptured lips formed her best ingenuous smile yet. "I guess it's beginning to rub off."

"Yeah, that's probably it."

He still looked puzzled, but maybe not as much as before.

"I couldn't help noticing that you're wearing cowboy boots and jeans," she said with a Texas accent.

"Were you raised on a farm? Or do you just like Western clothes?"

"A little of both, I guess. But it was a ranch. Not a farm," he corrected with a spark of amusement in his eyes. He glanced out the window. "Why, it's starting to sprinkle."

The light shower had turned to rain by the time she looked out too. The trees and the entire parking lot had grayed eerily. She could barely see the street beyond.

"You sure don't need to be out in wet weather with that cough of yours." He glanced toward the side door. "If you'll give me your car keys, I'll re-park your car under the carport."

"I—I walked."

"Walked? Didn't you notice those dark clouds coming up from the north?"

"I guess I was distracted. Coming from far west Texas, I'm still amazed when I find autumn colors this far south. Besides, fall is my favorite time of the year."

"Fall's my favorite time of the year too," he said. "But you need to look up once in a while, young lady. Know what I mean?"

Suzann forced herself to hold in a smile. Josh looked to be in his mid- to late-twenties. She was probably only a few years younger than he, if that.

"I'll try to remember to do that," she said after the long pause. "But I do hope you'll keep reminding me."

He cocked his head to one side and grinned his

heart-stopping smile again. "I can't seem to stop preaching, can I?"

"Occupational hazard, I guess."

He laughed. "You know, you have a great sense of humor. I guess I never saw that side of you before."

"My funny side only comes out when I'm feeling a little bit under the weather."

His animated expression fell away. "That's right. You're sick, aren't you?"

"I think I just need to rest up from my vacation."

"Well, if you think I'm going to let you walk home in the rain, you have another think coming." He reached in his pocket and pulled out a set of keys. "Let me pull my truck around. And meet me at the side entrance in five minutes." He started to walk off, then stopped and turned back. "Unless you would rather stay a little longer."

"No," she said. "I'm ready to go right now."

She knew she shouldn't be catching a ride with her sister's secret love. But it was raining outside. And she was feeling sicker by the minute.

Chapter Two

Holly, on her flight to California, tried to ignore Mike in the first-class seat beside her. Yet he kept staring at her as if he couldn't believe his eyes. He appeared amazed that she looked so much like Suzann. Holly had the sudden urge to stare right back.

With his green eyes and blond hair, some might call Mike McDowell handsome. Holly saw him as conceited, condescending and a big phoney. During the last two weeks, the only time he'd been halfway civil was when her sister was around.

A man like Mike probably expected every woman on the planet to fall down at his feet. He would be surprised if he knew how truly unimpressed Holly really was. She would definitely put Mike McDowell on her prayer list.

Suzann had depicted Mike as charming, a sweetheart. Holly thought his congenial attitude was a facade to impress her wealthy sister. She intended to be courteous to Mike, but the friendship balls were all in his court.

He leaned back in his seat and crossed his arms over his chest. "We'll be landing in less than a hour, and I'm bushed. I haven't had a day off in over two weeks. Sometimes I think Suzann forgets that she's not my only client."

Holly didn't feel like making a comment.

"I hope you don't mind," he continued, "but I'll be out of pocket for the next few days. So I won't be able to take your phone calls."

She stared at him, unable to believe what she was hearing. "What?"

"Now, hold on. Don't blow this way out of proportion. You can still call me—just not right away. And whatever you do, don't tell your sister."

"Now, let's see. I don't know a single person in California but you. And I'm pretending to be a movie star. So if a problem comes up, who should I call? Nine-one-one?"

He laughed. "That sounds like something Suzann would say. I'm glad to see that you're finally beginning to lighten up."

"And?"

"I have someone in mind to take my place. You can call him anytime." He handed her a calling card.

Stunned, Holly shook her head. Then she glanced down at the white card. Turning it over, she read a name and a phone number. Dr. Shawn McDowell, Pediatrician.

"Shawn's my younger brother," Mike said.

"Does he know who I am?"

"Not yet."

Her sister had said that nobody else in California was to know. But that was because Suzann assumed Holly could go to Mike for help. Did Mike intend to explain the situation to his brother? Or leave Holly dangling?

If his past history symbolized his future acts, Mike planned to wash his hands of the entire matter. So far, he'd showed a complete lack of interest in doing anything he was hired to do.

Holly was completely disillusioned long before her plane touched down at Los Angeles International. By the time the limo her sister rented arrived at Suzann's hilltop mansion in southern California, Holly felt like Alice at the bottom of an extremely majestic rabbit hole.

The house was done in shades of blue and off-white, suiting Holly's tastes perfectly. She found antiques in almost every room—from France, Germany, England. Pewter goblets and bowls were everywhere. If I'm ever as rich as my sister, she thought, I'll decorate my whole house just like this.

Gertie, her sister's round, jolly, Austrian house-keeper, and Gertie's son, Buddy, gave Holly a warm "Welcome home." But, of course, they thought she was Suzann. Bates, Suzann's butler, driver and some-times secretary, exhibited a more formal demeanor.

When phone calls from Suzann's numerous Holly-wood friends started pouring in, she told Bates to say she was unavailable. Holly wasn't ready to play "let's pretend."

Shortly before lunch, she picked up her Bible and

moved outdoors, settling into a reclining chair by the pool. She imagined what the pool might look like on a summer night, the blue water all lighted up and inviting. The surrounding lawn looked smooth and green, with rows of tropical plants lining the rustic, cedar fence.

The setting was lovely. However, she'd never felt lonelier nor more out of place. Her old life in Texas hadn't prepared her for the fast lane. For all the help her childhood experiences on a Texas ranch gave her, she might as well be living on another planet.

But she'd see this through, no matter what. Without the opportunity to spend time in a Bible-believing church environment, Suzann might never find the Lord.

She'd questioned whether or not she should phone Suzann and tell her about Mike. Sure, he'd asked Holly not to tell her sister that he wouldn't be taking her calls, but Holly never promised she wouldn't.

The unmistakable scent of cucumbers reminded her that she was hungry. She selected a sandwich from the tray Gertie placed beside her chair. The crunchy cucumber and taste of mayo fill her mouth. The sandwich was certainly palatable, but Holly would have preferred a cheeseburger and fries. She put down the sandwich and reached for her Bible.

After reading for half an hour, she prayed. Finally, she relaxed. She was about to close her eyes and take a quick nap when a man she didn't know opened the yard gate and started toward her.

Holly jerked to a sitting position.

The man looked to be in his early thirties. He

wasn't tall—probably not more than five-eight—and his close-cropped hairstyle framed a rugged-looking face that few would call handsome. Yet Holly saw a kindness in that face. Somehow with a simple glance, he managed to put her at ease.

"Where did you come from?" she asked.

"I'm sorry, Miss Condry, if I scared you. But my brother, Mike, asked me to stop by. Your maid said I'd find you here."

His deep voice was as comforting as his warm, open gaze.

Relief surged through her. "Oh, yes. He mentioned you." She forced a pleasant expression. "You're the pediatrician." She offered him her hand.

"I'm Shawn McDowell."

"Glad to know you, Doctor."

"Please, call me Shawn." He shrugged, clearly baffled, and shook his head. "Look, I don't have a clue what I'm doing here." Shawn peered at Holly as if he expected answers. "Would you mind filling me in?"

When she didn't reply, he raked his hand through his thick, sandy hair. Then he pulled up one of the benches and sat down beside her.

Holly was at a loss to know what to say. Wasn't it enough that Mike had deserted her? Did he also expect her to cover his tracks?

It would be easy to simply play along, pretend she was Suzann, and make Mike do his own dirty work. But that wasn't Holly's style. As a Christian, she felt she had to be honest with this man. His enquiring, blue-green eyes demanded it.

"I'm not who you think I am." Her throat tightened. She paused before continuing. "I thought Mike would have told you."

He scratched his head thoughtfully. "I must have missed something. I have no idea what you're talking about."

"I'm not Suzann Condry."

"What did you say?"

She lowered her lashes so she wouldn't have to see his reaction to her revelation. "I'm her identical twin sister, Holly Harmon."

"Look, ma'am, I think I'm in way over my head here." He stood as if to leave. "I better go."

She felt the color drain from her face. "No, please. Wait."

"I'm a doctor. Not a private detective. Mike should have sent a private investigator, instead."

Tears glistened in her eyes. First she'd convinced Suzann she should tell her parents in Texas about the identity switch. Now she'd told the secret again and still had no one to turn to.

One of her false eyelashes partially separated from her left eye. She yanked it off, pulling off the other one for good measure. The doctor probably found such behavior offensive, but she hated false anything. She also hated her current situation.

Holly knew the rules in Oak Valley. She had no idea how to proceed here. The urge to cry was now almost overwhelming.

"Don't go." Her voice choked with emotion. "I need…"

He sat down on the bench again. His compassionate gaze touched her emotionally. "Hey, are you all right?" He hesitated. "Is there someone you would like me to call?"

"There's nobody I can phone but your brother, and he's not taking my calls."

"How 'bout if we start at the beginning?" he suggested gently.

As best she could, Holly explained all that had happened in the last month. If his expression was an indication, Shawn McDowell wasn't buying any of it.

"Do you expect me to believe all this is on the level?"

"As strange as it may sound, I do."

"And you also want me to believe you're a church librarian?"

"Normally, I hardly wear makeup at all." She sniffed and wiped her eyes. "My hair's dark auburn, and I wear glasses."

A slow grin started in his eyes. "A sort of female Clark Kent, huh?"

She returned his smile and glanced down at her Bible. "Yeah."

"So what do you want me to do?"

"Your brother said you would fill in for him while he's—out of pocket. The trouble is, I don't know what he was supposed to do...besides take my phone calls and escort me around town."

"Phone calls, I can do. I'll check with my brother to learn my other duties."

"Then you're willing to help me?"

His grin held a trace of amusement. "I'll do whatever I can."

"Oh, thank you, Dr. McDowell."

"Shawn."

"You can't imagine how much I appreciate this. But if you don't mind, please call me Suzann." Her laugh held a nervous undertone. "I'm supposed to be an actress. Isn't that a riot?"

"I don't know. I think you're doing a pretty good job of it. You managed to convince me to go along with your plan, didn't you?"

"Oh, I'm so sorry to put you out like this."

"Don't be sorry." His smile caused Holly's heart to skip a beat. "I think I might learn to enjoy it."

Suzann reclined on the blue couch in Holly's living room. Since Josh drove her back to the apartment, she'd had a constant string of guests—concerned church members—bearing covered dishes of food. She appreciated their kindness, but she just wanted to be alone and get some sleep.

She'd tried her best to pay attention to her current visitor. For almost half an hour, Mrs. Henrietta Beesley had talked endlessly about her single nephew from Dallas.

"He's a preacher, you know," she'd said, "and a church librarian would be perfect for someone like him."

Mrs. Beesley rattled on. Suzann wondered what she was going to do with all that food; the dishes covered the kitchen table. Part would fit in the refrigerator. Some might go in the freezer. She had no idea what to do with the rest.

Maybe she would give it to Josh Gallagher. After

all, he was the one who must have spread the word around that she was ill.

Mrs. Beesley picked up her empty dessert plate and leaned toward the coffee table that separated them. She'd placed the chocolate cake she had brought directly in front of her and had already had two slices.

"I must say, this is the best cake I've ever made." She grinned sheepishly. "Would you mind terribly if I had another piece?"

"Not at all." Suzann choked back a laugh. "Help yourself."

The older woman cut a slice of cake. The doorbell rang.

The mere thought of facing anymore covered dishes made Suzann feel sick to her stomach. She cherished the concern and kindness of the church members she'd met. But enough was enough. She got up off the couch and crept to the door.

Josh Gallagher stood on the front porch, holding a paper bag. "How are you feeling?" He reached in the sack and pulled out a can of chicken soup. "How does soup and crackers sound to you?" he asked. "I'm buying."

She was surprised at how happy she was to see him. "Hi, Josh. Come in. Mrs. Beesley's here," she added with a nod toward the older woman—seated on the couch.

An embarrassed smile surfaced on Josh's handsome face. "Glad to see you, Mrs. Beesley," he said. "How's the back?"

Mrs. Beesley joined Suzann at the door. "Oh, Brother Gallagher." Eyes fluttering, the older woman pressed her hands together excitedly. "How kind of you to ask." Her bubbly expression faded, and she placed her right hand to the small of her back. "I've really been in a lot of pain lately."

Suzann focused her gaze on Josh as he listened intently to Mrs. Beesley describe her ailments. Casually, he turned to Suzann.

"Miss Harmon looks tired," Josh said to Mrs. Beesley. "Why don't we put away the food and let her get some rest?" He grinned at Suzann. "We'll lock the door on our way out."

Suzann hadn't meant to actually go to sleep. But that was an exceptionally downy couch. She drifted off in seconds.

When she opened her eyes, the telephone was ringing. She sat up. Someone had covered her with a blue, patchwork quilt. What a sweet thing to do, she thought. A smile played on her lips as she reached for the telephone.

"Hello?"

"Hi," Josh said. "How was the soup?"

"Soup?"

"The soup Mrs. Beesley and I left warming in your oven. Didn't you see my note?"

"Not yet, I just woke up."

She glanced out the double windows facing the street. It was already dark outside. She looked down for her watch and realized she wasn't wearing it.

"What time is it, anyway?" she asked.

"Six-thirty."

"I must have really slept."

"Apparently. Didn't you hear all that racket when the thunderstorm passed through?"

"Not a thing."

"So far, we've had almost half an inch of rain."

"Really?"

She knew he hadn't called to give her a weather report. Though she liked talking to him, she wished he would get to the point.

"Do you mind if I stop by and give you that music I promised?" he asked. "I ran it off on the machine here at the church a few minutes ago."

She wanted him to drop by, but...

"I'll just stay a minute," he added. "I'm headed for a movie, and you're on my way."

Did he have a date for the evening? It bothered her to realize that he might. The fact that she cared one way or the other worried her still more.

"What do you say? May I come by or not?"

"Sure," she heard herself say, "come on over."

"Can I get you anything from the store first? You know, something for your cold? Tissues, maybe? Throat lozenges?"

"Right now, I can't think of a thing."

"Then I'll see you in ten minutes."

Josh was coming on pretty fast and strong for a country preacher. But maybe he was just trying to be kind. Wasn't it part of his job? Why, half the congregation had stopped by to check on her that day.

Suzann cautioned herself not to attach any special meaning to Josh's concern. He was probably just a caring person.

Caring.

A picture of Greer Fraser's handsome face rose up before her. Suzann flinched. Greer had proved just how uncaring he really was the day he broke off their relationship and moved into Elaine Eaton's apartment in Los Angeles.

Holly would probably say she should never have gotten so involved with a man like Greer. But how could Holly possibly understand the kind of life Suzann had lived before she came to Oak Valley?

Suzann should never have allowed Greer back in her life, but he'd showed a renewed interest in her once he moved to California. Suzann fell for it. And why not? Greer was considered by some to be the best-looking man in Hollywood.

Until Greer, Suzann had always refused to date actors, convinced that they were too in love with themselves to truly love someone else. However, Greer seemed to have changed since New York City. Suzann had thought he was warmer—more honest.

The fact that he'd duped her the second time proved two things: his acting talent was greater than his critics indicated, and Suzann Condry could be deceived.

Loving and caring were just words to Suzann. The citizens of Oak Valley might believe in such things, and once, she did, too. But she was no longer convinced those romantic notions had any basis in reality.

A tickle in her throat became a deep cough. A knock at her door said that Josh waited on the porch outside. She took a sip of water to muffle her cough. It didn't work.

"You all right in there?" he asked. "That cough of yours sounds bad."

"Give me a minute. I'll be fine."

She fumbled in her purse for the cough drops he'd given her, then remembered that she'd left them in his truck. Her eyes watered and burned. Suzann wiped her eyes, took a big swallow of water, and coughed some more.

"Let me in this minute," he said. "Or I'll huff and I'll puff and I'll—"

"Okay, okay."

She stumbled to the door and nearly fell. Grabbing hold of the back of the high-backed rocker, she paused to steady herself.

She knew that she had been dizzy earlier, but hadn't counted on being weak as well. Suzann flipped the latch and stepped back from the door.

Josh's encouraging smile faded. "You need to see a doctor."

"It's just a cold. Besides, doctors' offices aren't open on Saturday night. Won't you come in?"

"The emergency room at the hospital over in Kerrville is open." He came inside, removed his raincoat, and looked around.

"Just drop your raincoat there, by the door."

Wrapping his wet coat in a tight tan bundle, he did as she said. His dark brown hair looked damp and curlier than she remembered. He handed her the sheet music wrapped in clear plastic. "Here." Then he shook out the surplus moisture from his hair. Droplets of rainwater trickled down both cheeks.

"I'll get you a towel."

"No, no, no. You sit. I'll get it."

"But you don't even know where the bathroom is."

"I'll find it."

"Through the bedroom. First door to the right."

Suzann felt self-conscious and blushy, but managed to hide it. She'd entertained men alone in her house many times. So why was she embarrassed now? Was she suddenly becoming another Pollyanna like her sister?

In six months she would leave God, the church, and the state of Texas forever. Her goal was to learn from these people, not join them. She was in Oak Valley to rest and sample a normal life. And for no other reason.

She'd done background studies for various movie roles in the past. Why was this any different? She would simply have to become more objective.

Josh trekked back to the living room, rubbing his head with a blue towel. Suzann had settled onto the couch again. He sat down beside her.

"I hope you don't catch my cold," she said.

"Not a chance. I just had one." He wrinkled his nose boyishly. "And that's my quota for the year." He grinned. "Besides, I've been praying."

"I hope it helps." *Why did I say that?* she wondered. "I mean—" she shrugged "—of course it helps."

"Nobody would know that better than a prayer warrior like you."

Prayer warrior? What's that?

Nothing came to mind. If Holly mentioned that

subject at all, it had been deleted from her brain before Suzann arrived in Oak Valley. She would need to phone Holly and asked her for a definition of these new terms.

"You know," he said, "we're expecting more rain tomorrow. I don't think you should even consider trying to go to church in the morning unless you feel a lot better."

He slanted his head to one side, pressing his palm against her forehead. A thrill shot through her.

"You have fever. Have you eaten anything?"

"Not yet, but I will."

"I haven't eaten anything since lunch," he said. "How about if we pull out that soup from the oven, open the crackers, and have us a feast? Otherwise, I'll be stuck eating a bucket of popcorn at the movie."

"Soup and crackers sounds good to me."

Since it was her home, Suzann expected to serve the meal. But Josh insisted on doing all the work. As he set about laying the table and fixing the food, he urged her to take something for her fever and even went to the medicine cabinet in the bathroom in search of aspirin.

Suzann had never known a man that could be so nurturing and at the same time so manly. She found the combination delightful. Suzann grew reflective. Holly had expressed those same sentiments about Josh.

When Josh returned to the kitchen, he brought a yellow rose from the bouquet Mrs. Winslow had sent. He placed the flower in a china bud vase on the small table. Sitting across from her, Josh folded his big, rough hands, and said the blessing.

Later, as they spooned their soup, Suzann took in the white linen table cloth and her sister's spotless kitchen. The table looked lovely. Josh had thought of everything. They were even using linen napkins and Holly's best china.

"Everything looks perfect," she said. "I feel like a queen. But you've done too much. If this keeps up, you'll have me spoiled."

"Sick people deserve to be spoiled."

"You're very kind. In fact, the whole congregation is kind. Maybe too kind. I've never seen so much food in all my life."

"I've talked to several of the ladies since they stopped by to see you, and you're well-liked here in Oak Valley. But I suppose you know that."

She glanced down at her soup bowl. "Thanks again."

He put down his spoon and wiped his mouth. "Mrs. Winslow mentioned that you insisted on seeing pictures of all her grandchildren. Do you like children?"

"Yes. I mean— Of course I do."

Suzann liked children, all right, but that was not the reason she'd asked to see the pictures. She was still trying to match names with faces.

"Have you ever worked with children, Miss Harmon?" he asked.

"Yes. And please, call me—call me Holly." Suzann blinked, trying to think how her sister would have responded. Nothing surfaced. Was she about to blow her cover?

"Maybe you shouldn't call me Holly after all," she said.

"Why not?"

"It sounds too informal."

"As you must know, many in the church even call the pastor by his first name."

"That's true but…"

"You think I should call you Miss Harmon."

"Exactly."

"All right," he said, and a faint smile shone through. "But it seems out of character for you."

"Out of character? Why?"

"Now that I've gotten to know you, you seem more down to earth than the shy librarian I first thought you were."

"The change is only temporary. As I said earlier, I'll be my old self again as soon as I get over this cold."

He chuckled softly under his breath. "Frankly, I like you better the way you are now."

"Coughing and sneezing my head off?"

He threw back his head and laughed. "No, that's not what I meant at all." His mirthful laugh evolved into something much more intense. "I think you know it too."

Was she imagining things? Or did that look in his eyes say that he found her extremely attractive?

This would never do. She shouldn't have allowed Josh to drop by again, much less fix her supper. It was probably something Holly would never have considered doing.

She glanced at the clock over the refrigerator. "It's ten after seven. If you don't leave right now, you'll be late for that movie."

"I'm already late," he said. "The movie starts in five minutes. I could never get there in time. But that's okay. The picture is there for three more nights and—" he studied her painstakingly "—you're tired, aren't you?"

"Well, it has been a long day." She faked a coughing spell to make her point.

"You go in and rest while I do these dishes."

"Please. Don't." Suzann hadn't intended to sound so abrupt. She tried to soften it by forcing a weak smile. "Put the dishes in the sink to soak. I'll do them later."

"Sure, and then I'm out of here." He paused contemplatively. "Do you mind if I phone you in the morning to see how you're doing?"

"Go ahead if you like, but I can't promise I'll answer. I'm taking your advice and sleeping in."

"I won't call until after church then," he said.

"That's very thoughtful of you, but don't feel that you must. I do a pretty good job of taking care of myself."

His face flashed disappointment. "I see." Josh continued to study her with those electrifying blue eyes of his.

She felt terrible for speaking so curtly to him. Suzann wished she could take back her sharp remark. Yet if she did, he might miss her meaning.

Josh slipped his right hand in the pocket of his jeans as if he was searching for his truck keys. "I better go," he said rigidly, "and I hope that cold of yours disappears real soon."

"Thanks."

Then he left.

She hadn't liked treating him so callously. Suzann bit her lower lip.

Like many child actors, Suzann had always felt that in order to get love and acceptance, one must perform perfectly—before the camera and everywhere else. She had no faith in people who offered affection without expecting something in return.

Suzann knew she was still slightly depressed over her breakup with Greer Fraser. Until the onset of her cold, she hadn't realized that she was physically exhausted as well. When Josh offered to nurse her back to health, Suzann was warmed by his concern and amazed at how different he was from Greer and the other men she'd dated in the past.

Somehow, Josh's interest and nurturing nature struck an unsung chord deep within her—as if he was gently teaching her to trust. At the same time, Suzann saw Josh's kindness as a warning. Take it slow and easy. Men like Josh were rare in California...and that was where she would be living in six months.

She knew she needed the kind of tenderness and understanding that Josh could give her. But she was afraid to reach out and take it. Besides, she wasn't in Oak Valley to start a romance. Or to steal her sister's beau.

Chapter Three

Suzann crawled into Holly's single bed under the double windows and went right to sleep. Four hours later, she woke up, feeling uneasy and slightly disoriented, but fully awake.

Yawning, she glanced at the luminous clock, blinking in the darkness. Eleven o'clock.

It would be nine in California. Maybe she should give her sister a call.

Suzann fumbled for the phone on the nightstand, then dialed. Bates answered. *Rats.* She'd hoped Holly would pick up. She faked her best Spanish accent ever and asked to speak with Miss Condry.

"She's talking to a gentleman in the drawing room."

Suzann's right brow lifted. "Really? Tell her this is Maria Garcia from Texas. Her friend from Oak Valley."

"She hasn't been taking her calls today. But if you'll hold, I'll go in and give her your message."

Suzann coughed. "Thanks."

A few minutes later Holly came on the line.

"Your Spanish accent must have been pretty convincing," Holly said. "You sure had your butler fooled."

"It's not the first time. How's—" Suzann coughed again "—how's California?"

"Super, but you don't sound so good. Are you all right?"

"Just a slight cold. So, how do you like my humble abode?"

"Your house is fabulous. But if you hadn't drawn me that map, I would never have found your bedroom."

Suzann smiled. "Who's your guest? Mike?"

Holly grew silent. "No, his brother."

"The pediatrician?"

"Yeah."

"Mike said his brother had moved to Burbank. So what's Shawn doing there? And where's Mike?"

"It's a little hard to explain right now. And Shawn—I mean, Dr. McDowell—is waiting. Could I call you back tomorrow?"

"Sure."

Suzann held the receiver away from her ear for a moment before hanging up. Something strange was going on in California. She intended to find out what it was.

Suzann slept late the next morning. She might have slept longer, but a coughing episode woke her. When she recovered, she got out of bed and fixed herself a cup of coffee.

The church members she'd met would be in Sunday School and then church. So would Josh. She was free to study Holly's family photo album and the pictorial *Church Directory.*

At a little before twelve, she fell asleep again. She didn't open her eyes until she heard another knock.

Suzann combed her fingers through her hair and made her way to the door, pulling her white, terry-cloth robe closed in front as she went. The small window above the door revealed a young woman about Suzann's age. She'd noticed her picture in the *Church Directory.* Still in her groggy state, she couldn't remember her name.

Suzann opened the door. "Excuse my appearance—and for looking so vacant. But I've been sleeping a lot with this cold of mine." She slanted her head to one side. "Please, come in."

The young woman frowned briefly as if she might be confused. She was short and petite. Her hair was darker than Suzann's. Some might call it black. Her eyes were a warm gray and circled by a thick layer of black lashes.

"We missed you at church this morning."

"I missed being there."

Suzann motioned toward the couch, taking the chair to the right of the couch for a better view of her guest. Could this be her neighbor? Suzann had caught a glimpse of a neighbor when Josh drove her home, but that woman had looked slightly older. So who?

In hopes of appearing relaxed and casual, Suzann

pulled up her legs, covered them with her white robe, and hugged her knees.

"What's been going on in Oak Valley since I've been gone?" Suzann asked.

The young woman sent her another puzzled expression, as if she'd expected Suzann to say something entirely different.

"Are you sure you're all right, Holly?" the young woman asked. "You seem a little—" she shook her head "—I don't know…different."

Suzann stretched out her legs and sat up. Her body language earlier wasn't doing the job. It was time for Plan B. Too bad she hadn't come up with one yet.

"Maybe you should see a doctor or something," the woman said. "About that cold, I mean."

"That's what half the church members who came by here yesterday said."

"I would have come by yesterday too but— I just got back late last night."

"How was your trip?"

"Trip?"

Suzann tensed. *Trip* was obviously not the word she should have used with this particular person. Wake up, Suzann, she thought. She could always blame her present addled state on her fever.

"That wasn't a very good choice of words, was it?" Suzann said. "Sorry. How did it go?"

"At first Mother was devastated, of course. But she's better, now that we think Dad's going to be all right."

"We can thank God for that." Suzann suddenly

realized to whom she was speaking, and her heart went out to Kate Devlon.

"I'm sorry about your dad," Suzann said softly. "Wish I could have been there for you."

"There was no reason for you to disrupt your vacation, and there was nothing you could do. Besides, you phoned, didn't you?"

Suzann nodded. She should have guessed that the stranger was Holly's best friend the minute Kate walked in.

Holly had described Kate as warm and fun-loving. Had Suzann known to whom she was speaking, common sense would have told her that Kate wasn't likely to be upbeat when her father had just suffered a heart attack.

"You probably need to get back in bed." Kate stood. "I better leave."

Suzann wanted her to stay. However, it might be best to wait until she felt a little better and could keep up her Holly act before they had a prolonged visit.

Suzann got up then. "I'm really glad you stopped by."

"Me too." Kate grinned before starting for the door. "I would have brought you a covered dish, but—" she laughed and turned back to Suzann "—Brother Josh said that maybe you would like a visit only."

Suzann followed Kate to the door. "He's very perceptive."

"Isn't he, though?" Kate winked. "Do I smell romance in the air?"

"Romance?" Suzann was caught off guard by

Kate's remark. "No." She shrugged nonchalantly. "We just happen to work at the same church, that's all."

"Are you sure that's all it is?"

Suzann opened her mouth to answer. Then closed it. It would be too easy to say the wrong thing.

When Kate had gone, Suzann went back to the couch and reached for the *Church Directory*. She hoped to recall everything Holly said about Kate Devlon. She remembered that Kate was a rancher's daughter, turned secretary to a local lawyer, and that she moved to Oak Valley about the same time Josh did. If Suzann hoped to be a convincing Holly Harmon, she would need to stay as close to Kate as possible.

By nightfall Suzann was beginning to question whether or not Holly intended to return her call. Josh hadn't phoned either, but she wasn't surprised after what she'd said to him.

At eight o'clock—California time—Suzann phoned Holly. Bates informed her that Miss Condry went out to dinner with Dr. McDowell. Confused and slightly aggravated, Suzann phoned Mike.

"I'm sorry," a female at his answering service said, "but Mr. McDowell is out of the country. Why not try him again early next week?"

Out of the country?

Mike was hired to escort Holly around the area. What was he doing out of the country? His answering service wasn't willing to give her so much as his location or a phone number.

Suzann phoned Holly again, instructing Bates to tell Miss Condry to call Maria Garcia no matter how late it was when she came in.

She'd drifted off to sleep when the phone rang.

"What's the matter?" Holly asked. "Is your cold worse?"

"No, I was worried about you. And Mike's out of the country. Would you mind telling me what's going on?"

"Mike went on—on a sort of vacation."

"So I heard," said Suzann sarcastically.

"He said he was tired from two weeks in Texas without a day off. So he sent his brother to fill in until he gets back."

"Does Shawn know who you really are?"

"I had to tell him, under the circumstances. Sorry," Holly replied.

"It wasn't your fault. But wait until I get my hands on Mike." Suzann coughed several times. "How is Shawn working out as Mike's stand-in?"

"Fine. In fact, I like him better than Mike."

"But your heart belongs to Josh Gallagher, right?"

"Suzann, I wish you'd stop saying that. Josh Gallagher has hardly said ten words to me since the day we met. Besides, I heard he's got a girlfriend who lives near that ranch his parents own, somewhere in the northern part of the hill country. And Mrs. Beesley said that his parents hope he'll marry her someday."

Suzann tried to swallow what Holly had said. But it would take time to digest it all.

"Are you still on the line?" Holly asked.

"I'm here. So what's Shawn like? I've never met him."

"Well, he's warm, friendly, easy to talk to. He's not pretty-boy handsome like his older brother. But in my opinion, he's much better looking."

"This sounds serious," she teased.

"I just met the man *yesterday*," Holly said with a sigh. "He only asked me out because he felt sorry for me after the way Mike treated me."

"Maybe I should hire Shawn to look after you instead of Mike."

"Don't you dare because a man like Shawn McDowell has scruples. He might be insulted. Besides, he's a Christian."

"Excellent. This is getting better by the second."

"The man is only being kind, Suzann. Why can't you understand that?"

Suzann's laughter echoed back to her. "We'll see. Won't we?"

"I don't like the sound of your laugh. And if it means you're planning to hire Shawn, I'll never speak to you again."

"Don't worry. I was only joking. But if I contribute to the building of the new pediatric wing he plans to help build for poor children, who would be the wiser?"

Suzann felt a lot better after talking to Holly. Now she knew for sure that her sister had no claim on or interest in Josh Gallagher. But what about the girlfriend Holly mentioned? Was Josh serious about her?

If so, what business was it of Suzann's? It would be a bigger stretch than she could fathom to think that a country preacher and a movie star might become a twosome. She needed to forget Josh Gallagher and focus on her real reasons for coming to Oak Valley, Texas.

Suzann returned to Holly's job at the church library on Wednesday. Three women stopped by to check out books. Suzann liked them, but with the women mentioning the name *Jesus* in practically every sentence, her problem was in relating to them.

The church secretary burst into the library. Suzann secretly winced, then made an earnest effort to smile. Holly had said that Mrs. Olson was demanding but had a kind heart—once you got to know her. All she needed to do was get to know the woman as soon as possible.

"Here's a schedule of events for the rest of the week," the elderly secretary said. "Prayer meeting's tonight at 6:30 p.m., followed by choir practice. Tomorrow night the women's Bible study is at seven. You'll be attending as usual, of course?"

Was she kidding?

"Friday night," Mrs. Olson continued, "a school is scheduled for those who'll be teaching Fall Vacation Bible School this year. I see you're on the list."

"I am? I mean—I certainly am."

"And don't worry about the library. We'll close the library during that whole week, just like we did last year."

"That's good news." Suzann couldn't believe what she was hearing. Was there such a thing as a night off around here?

"And don't forget that you promised to help with the bake sale and car wash on Saturday to raise money for the church youth group," Mrs. Olson added. "It'll be held on the church parking lot again. And I hope you don't mind teaching your Sunday School class this Sunday. Sally Rogers is out of town."

"I'll—I'll be glad to do—to do whatever."

"I was sure you would be. And remember to bring one of those delicious cakes of yours to the bake sale, Saturday."

Suzann blinked. "Cake?"

"But with your talent for baking, just any cake you want to bring will be fine."

Suzann had never baked a cake in her entire life. Nor had she taught a Sunday School class. Ditto to Vacation Bible School. She was thankful that the church secretary had left a copy of her duties. Otherwise, she would never remember them all. The thought of actually doing them made her head swim.

Okay, so she knew before she arrived in Oak Valley that Holly was a Christian and the church librarian. How could she have known that Holly's entire life was immersed in the church?

Suzann didn't see Josh again until the Vacation Bible School meeting on Friday night. The pastor was involved elsewhere. Josh conducted the meeting.

She sat stiffly beside Kate Devlon in the second row, speculating about whether or not Josh intended to acknowledge her. He'd made it clear that he wanted nothing more to do with her, and that seemed like a strange attitude for the youth director and assistant pastor of a church.

"Did you and Brother Josh have a spat?" Kate asked.

"Spat? Why, he means nothing to me."

"Maybe not, but I think you mean something to him."

Suzann wanted to remind Kate that Josh Gallagher had a girlfriend back home. She never got the chance.

A hush permeated the room. Josh asked Brother Winslow to lead the group in prayer.

Josh couldn't help seeing Suzann during the meeting, but he acted as if she were invisible. The way he deliberately avoided her gaze exasperated her.

"See what I mean?" Kate whispered.

Suzann rolled her eyes upward.

Josh might never have looked at her if Suzann hadn't raised her hand in answer to one of his questions.

"Yes, Miss Harmon," he said without expression. "What kind of refreshments would you suggest for snack time?"

"Snow cones would be nice. They're easy to fix, and if it turns cold again, we could serve hot chocolate instead."

"That's an interesting idea," he said, "but I understand we had that last year. I'd like to try something new." He looked away. "Anyone else?"

One of ladies who came into the library on Wednesday raised her hand. "Well, I like Miss Harmon's idea about the snow cones. Just because we had them last year doesn't mean we can't have them again, and the children really seemed to like them.''

"I second that,'' Kate said.

Josh's mouth tightened. "Then if nobody has any other ideas, I guess it's snow cones again.'' He glanced at Suzann indifferently. "Thanks for the suggestion.''

She nodded, looking down at her teacher's manual.

"So if nobody has anything else to say,'' Josh said, "I guess I'll see y'all here Monday morning at eight o'clock, sharp, ready to teach our autumn version of Vacation Bible School. Oh, and don't forget the bake sale in the morning.''

Kate groaned. "How could we forget?''

Suzann stuck close to Kate's side as they walked out to the parking lot. She had no illusions that Josh Gallagher planned to seek her out. Still, it was nice to know that she wouldn't have to face him alone if he did.

Josh went straight to his truck, got in, and slammed the door behind him.

"Wow,'' Kate said. "He's got it bad.''

Suzann shook her head. "What Brother Josh has is a bad temper.''

"He never had it until you came back from vacation. I've never seen him like this, and I've known him all my life.''

"All your life?''

"Had you forgotten that we grew up together?'' Kate asked.

Could Kate Devlon be the girlfriend back home

whom she'd heard so much about? No, if she'd been Josh's girlfriend, Holly would have mentioned it.

"Would you like to go out for hamburgers?" Kate asked. "The Dizzy Dairy should be open, and I've got time, if you do."

"Hamburgers sounds great."

"Let's take my car."

Suzann had already learned that the Dizzy Dairy, or the "D.D." as it was sometimes called, was the only place in town that served hamburgers, except for Juan's Mexican Café. Kate drove by the D.D. slowly. Sure enough, Josh's truck was parked out front.

"I think I'd rather eat at Juan's," Suzann said.

"Are you chicken, or what?"

"Let's just say I'm playing it safe."

It was ten by the time Suzann got back to the apartment, and she still had a cake to bake. She opened the kitchen cabinet. A box of cake mix and a can of ready-made icing glared back at her. Grabbing both of them, she read the directions on the back of the cartons. Hmm, this sounds easy, she thought. Literally, a piece of cake.

Yes, baking appeared easy enough—until she smelled burning batter. Suzann raced into the kitchen, grabbed a potholder, and opened the oven. A big puff of smoke caused her eyes to water.

Coughing, she pulled her cake from the oven amid a cloud of smoke. Besides being scorched on the bottom, it was lopsided and had an odor that would kill a healthy horse.

She considered tossing the horrible flop in the garbage and defrosting one of the cakes in the freezer.

She might have if she'd thought she could get away with it.

Instead, she decided to tell the truth. So she burned a cake... What could they do to her? Even Mrs. Henrietta Beesley probably burned cakes once in a while.

A dry chill hung in the air the next morning as Suzann dressed for the bake sale. In jeans and a white, long-sleeved shirt, she added a green plaid jacket to cut the north wind that was howling outside.

She arrived at the parking lot right on time. A line of card tables were set up to the left of the white-painted, country church. Josh, in jeans, boots and a blue cowboy shirt, checked his watch. She assumed that he thought she was late.

Suddenly, it dawned on Suzann that she and Josh were the only ones there. Where were the youth group members? Where was Kate when she needed her?

"Kate called in sick." He examined her suspiciously without cracking a smile, his tan Stetson set firmly on his head. "Something about eating greasy burgers last night."

"I thought we were here to raise money so the kids can take a ski trip to Colorado during spring break."

His blue eyes narrowed. "We are."

"So where are they? Aren't the kids interested enough to help out?"

"The teenagers are on the parking lot at the back of the church building, washing cars. Of the two, I thought you might like helping with this job."

"You were right about that."

His guarded expression slackened. She thought he was on the brink of a smile.

"It's just the two of us this morning," he said. "Think you can handle it?"

"I don't see why not."

The muscles in his face relaxed. "So, how have you been?"

"Fine. My cold's almost gone."

"Took care of things all by yourself, did you?"

"I'm the oldest and the only girl in my family. Growing up, taking care of myself went with the territory."

"Think you're pretty independent, huh?" he said mockingly.

"I'm no clinging vine, if that's what you mean." Suzann went over to the card tables and began rearranging the pies. "There's not much here."

"It's early yet. People will be bringing stuff in all morning. By the way, what did you bring?"

She swallowed. "I...baked a cake."

"Great, where is it?"

"I'm getting to that." The wind whipped her hair, covering one of her eyes. "I just—" she pushed away the assailing strand of auburn hair "—I just didn't bring it."

"Why not?"

"I burned it, okay?"

"The famous Miss Harmon, baker extraordinaire, burned a cake? The young lady who has her recipes printed in the church cookbook? I can't believe it."

Suzann frowned. "Believe it."

"I thought you were supposed to be a prize-winning baker."

"I never said that."

"Everybody else did."

Suzann gazed at the card tables again. "Would you mind helping me move these tables? I think there would be more room for parking if we moved them a little closer to the building. It would also protect us from the wind."

"Whatever the lady wants."

An assortment of pastries had been brought to the church parking lot by noon. Suzann stood behind the table they were using as a counter top, surveying cakes, pies and cookies of all kinds.

The sweet scent of apple pie yanked her back to her childhood, flooding her mind with memories of a TV commercial she had made for a pastry company when she was seven. Suzann remembered the blinding yellow lights, and how hot and uncomfortable they made her feel.

The director had said in a loud voice, "Whatever you do, Mrs. Condry, don't let that kid of yours sweat. It'll ruin that expensive dress she's wearing."

Suzann had held her body stiff the way her mother told her for what seemed like hours, hoping to keep her body dry. But moisture trickled down her neck anyway, dampening the back of the yellow-organdy dress. The dress must have been saturated in starch. She'd thought it was pretty until she learned that the stiff organdy collar scratched her neck when she turned her head so much as an inch.

She could see the sterling-silver fork she used in the taping session as if it had happened yesterday. The filigreed fork had felt heavy in her hand and cold. Yet when she touched it to the pie, the spicy aroma of apples and cinnamon had bubbled up in a cloud of steam.

She recalled how she'd fantasized about the sweet sugary taste of it, assuming that the director would give her a slice when the session ended. But she wasn't given one bite of that apple pie. Even now, it hurt to think about it.

Josh sidled up beside her, propelling Suzann back to the present.

"Mrs. Beesley and several of the other ladies are going to relieve us so we can have some lunch," he said. "I'm going to the Dizzy Dairy. Would you like to come along?"

Suzann swallowed, still too caught up in her reflections to think of anything else. She needed a moment to shift gears.

Apparently, Josh and Holly weren't an item. Yet there was that girlfriend back home to consider, if there was such a woman.

She should probably refuse his offer, but she hated to turn him down. When he looked at her with that certain softness in his gaze—trying to act as if it didn't matter at all to him, and yet, it clearly did— she just couldn't say no. And she had to admit that she would enjoy his company.

"All right," she said, "as long as we go Dutch."

"Sounds good to me."

* * *

The Dizzy Dairy was crowded with kids. Some of them were children Suzann saw in church on Wednesday night.

"Hey, Brother Josh," a freckle-faced boy of about ten said. "Is that your girl?"

Josh grinned. "Eat your ice-cream cone, Robby, before it melts."

A slow smile formed on Suzann's lips. "Is that the way the assistant pastor—slash—youth director answers questions?"

"It depends on the questions."

"Okay, youth director, do you have a girl?"

"Maybe. How about you?"

Amused by his question, she couldn't keep from smiling, even though she chose not to answer.

"Let me put it to you another way, then." Humor danced in his eyes. "Are you seeing anyone right now?"

"No." Suzann pretended to study her menu so he wouldn't know she was valiantly holding back her laughter. "I think I'll have the taco salad. What are you going to have?"

"You're good at changing the subject, aren't you?"

After they returned to the parking lot, two overweight young boys on bikes wheeled over and stopped.

"They're the Howard brothers," Josh whispered. "Glen and Ben. Prepare for the worst."

"Robby Sullivan said that you're sweet on Miss Harmon," the taller boy said. "Is that true?"

"You better check with Robby, Ben. He seems to be the only one who knows anything around here."

Brother Winslow and his wife pulled up to drop off a pan of cookies.

Glen feigned a swooning spell when Mrs. Winslow walked by. "Man," he said, "chocolate chip. My favorite."

"Mine too," Ben added. "Can we have—?"

"No." Josh shook his head. "Not unless you show me your money first."

"But—" Ben shrugged.

"That's the deal, guys. No money, no cookies."

Ben pulled out the pockets of his jeans, proving that they were empty. "I left my billfold at home."

"In that case, we might be able to make a deal," Josh said. "I'll give you each a cookie if you'll tell everybody you see about the bake sale today."

"Well, all right." Ben slapped his younger brother's open palm, using the give-me-five sign.

When the boys had eaten their cookies, they licked their fingers down to the last possible crumb.

"Here." Suzann shook her head, handing each boy a paper napkin. "Try this. And don't forget to throw your napkins in the trash can before you leave."

The boys saluted her.

Amused, Suzann returned their salute. She watched them wipe their hands, nodding her approval when they tossed the napkins into the trash.

The two bikers started off again. They had almost reached the street when Ben stopped and turned back. "We sure thank you for the cookies, Brother Josh." He nodded to Suzann. "You too, Miss Harmon."

"Yeah, thanks," Glen tacked on.

"Glad to do it," Josh said. "We needed to advertise."

Ben giggled. "But you know what?"

"What?" Josh answered in a light tone.

"I still think Miss Harmon is your girlfriend." Then the boys raced away on their bicycles, laughing.

Suzann shook her head again and glanced at Josh.

He threw his head back in a heartfelt laugh. Josh's optimistic approach to life rubbed off, taking control of her funny bone. She found herself returning his smile.

Life in the small town of Oak Valley reminded her of a movie set in the forties or fifties. The difference was that a movie is make-believe. This was all too real.

Chapter Four

Suzann returned from the bake sale at three o'clock. The cool, brisk morning had become a warm, sunshiny Saturday afternoon. She changed into walking shorts and a green T-shirt.

If she thought Oak Valley was like an old movie, the bake sale was like stepping back in time. However, she knew she wouldn't want a steady diet of old movies—or Josh Gallagher. So why did Josh seem so appealing?

To get her mind off Josh, she gazed out her bedroom window at the hill directly behind her apartment. That particular hill had beckoned since the day she arrived in Oak Valley. Today she would climb to the top no matter what church duties she might have to postpone in order to do it.

Red oaks, mountain cedars and spiny underbrush spotted the rocky soil. Minor cuts and scratches appeared on her legs as she began her climb. Suzann didn't care that a mosquito buzzed about her head, because she was finally experiencing somewhat of a normal life. She slapped the mosquito, but not before it had taken a bite out of her arm.

Undeterred, she pushed on.

Farther up, tiny streams of springwater from the recent rains dampened the trail ahead. As she looked on, the streams trickled down to the bottom of the hill. Next time she would know to wear long pants, old shoes, and carry plenty of mosquito spray.

The view from the top of the hill spurred her imagination. Was this what was meant by "the other side of the mountain"?

What looked like tiny trees and miniature houses drifted downward in neat rows to the valley below. Through her binoculars, she also saw a small wooden church and quaint shops.

She intended to explore the shops one day soon. Perhaps she'd even give the church a look-see as well. For now, the hills summoned.

Suzann sat on the moist grass, feasting on the beauty of nature in all its fall grandeur. Yellow, rust, gold, red, orange, brown. They were all there—as if a painter had taken a huge brush, dipped it in color, and sprinkled autumn hues over the landscape.

Her sister would say that the artist was God. Suzann wanted to believe that too. She just couldn't. Simple answers wouldn't solve the complex problems of the modern world. Yet somehow, deep down, she wished that they would.

By the time she started down again, the cuts, scratches and bites looked red and irritated. She itched all over. Had she stepped in poison ivy?

Josh waited halfway down the hill. She'd have to walk right by him. Suzann closed her eyes, briefly, and sucked in her breath. What was *he* doing there?

Josh waved. Suzann peered down at her muddy shoes, hoping to discourage him. When she looked up again, an amused twinkle shone in his eyes.

"How was your hike?"

"Couldn't be better." Unconsciously, she scratched a bite on the back of her neck.

"Chiggers? Mosquitos? Or both?"

What are chiggers? she wondered.

"I would have thought," he said, "that a Texas girl like you would know how to protect herself against chigger bites."

She released a bored sigh. "Any medical tips you'd like to share?"

"I keep a bottle of pink lotion in the glove compartment of my truck that works pretty well. Would you like to try it?"

"Frankly at this point, I'll try anything."

He laughed. "I'll get the lotion and meet you back at your apartment."

"Fine, and by the way," she said, "what are you doing here anyway?"

"I have a message for you. But it can wait until you've applied the lotion." He turned and trudged back down the hill.

Suzann hurried back to the apartment house, hoping to arrive before Josh did. But he was waiting at the top of the outdoor stairway leading to the second floor, by the time she arrived. She resisted the urge to scratch both her legs as she joined him on her wooden porch.

"You're pretty chewed up." A glint flickered in his eyes. Then he handed her the lotion. "Would you like me to phone one of the women from our church to help you apply this stuff?"

"I can manage." She took the bottle from him feeling fortunate to know such a thoughtful person. "Thanks. I just hope this works."

"It'll work all right. But only for a little while."

"Then what do I do?"

"Dot yourself with the lotion again." His animated facial expression indicated that perhaps he enjoyed her discomfort. "But if you plan to continue walking in tall grass like you did today," he added, "I'd suggest you get some garlic pills at a health food store. Chiggers aren't likely to bite if you've just had one of those pills."

"Thanks again." Did one swallow the pills or rub them on the body? She was too embarrassed to ask. "I'll be sure to buy some of those pills. That's for sure."

She knew she should invite him in. But she'd promised herself that she wouldn't. Moreover, she wanted to soak in a warm bath for at least an hour.

"Thanks for all your help."

"Don't mention it." He took her hand and squeezed it. "Don't forget, we promised Pastor Jones we'd do that duet in church. Think you'll be up to it by next Sunday?" He grinned. "That's eight days from now."

"Well, I don't know." Suzann simulated a coughing spell.

"Would you like to put it off a little longer?"

"Could we?"

"Sure."

The way he kept staring at her lips hinted that he wanted to kiss her. Yet he turned and went back down the stairs.

Josh Gallagher was the perfect gentleman—like a man from a different era. And why not? According to what she'd heard, Josh grew up on a ranch with loving parents and was a typical, Bible Belt, conservative Christian.

"Brother Josh loves God," Mrs. Beesley said. "And he also loves people, the outdoors, and life in general."

Kate had stated almost the same thing on the night they ate hamburgers at Juan's Mexican Café.

"What I like best about Josh," Kate had said, "is that he's so honest, so caring, so loyal, and so much fun to be with. And if that's not enough, he was an Eagle Scout and won a good-citizen scholarship in high school."

In spite of her discomfort, Suzann stood watching him an instant longer. If Josh had decided to become an actor instead of a preacher, he would have made the perfect romantic hero.

A smile turned up the corners of her mouth. *Wow.* She heaved a deep sigh. Then she hurried inside.

She'd pulled off her shorts and removed her green shirt before she reached the bathroom. Turning on the tap, she stepped into the tub. Then she remembered that Josh never did deliver that message to which he referred.

The warm water felt good to her tired muscles. However, it seemed to activate the little red specks that were scattered all over her body, causing more itching. This would not be a long, soaking bath after all.

Twenty minutes later, Suzann sat on the couch in her living room, reading the dictionary. She'd dotted her entire body with pink lotion and turned the heating unit on high. She was shoeless and wearing just a two-piece, yellow bathing suit.

Chigger, she read. *The tiny larvae of certain mites that burrow under the skin.* She was about to read more when the phone rang.

"May I speak to Spot, please?" Josh said.

"Very funny."

"How did the pink stuff work?"

"Fine. Except I think it's time to put more on."

"That bad, huh?"

"Is this something the youth director and the church librarian should be discussing? And you never did deliver that message you mentioned."

"Then I'll get right to the point. Someone called the church this afternoon, looking for you. I just happened to be in the office when the call came in."

"Who would be calling me there?"

"Someone by the name of Maria Garcia, I believe."

Holly. But why would she be calling me at the church? "Did she leave a message?"

"She said she'd been trying to get you on the

phone. And I can believe it. After I hung up from talking to Maria, I tried to get you on the phone and couldn't. That's why I finally just came over. Maria said she thought your telephone must be out of order. But obviously, it's working all right now."

"Obviously."

"So," he said, sounding lighthearted, "how would you like to go out for Mexican food tonight? I can guarantee that Juan puts plenty of garlic in his chili sauce in case we might meet up with a nest of chiggers along the way."

Suzann wanted to say yes. She truly enjoyed his company and if she turned him down, she knew she'd just sit there thinking about him. Still, she hesitated to get any more involved with him.

"I—I can't. Not with pink dots all over me."

"Some other time then?"

"Sure."

His voice had lost most of its sparkle. She really liked Josh and hoped her "sure" hadn't sounded too much like a brush-off. She feared that it had.

Suzann finally got Holly on the phone. Ironically, Holly, speaking as Maria Garcia, said she'd just picked up the phone to try Suzann's number again. Suzann attributed this to the twin thing, but refrained from pointing that out to her sister.

Holly said she'd been unable to find Suzann's car keys, and Suzann told Holly where to find them. Their short conversation ended then, but not before Suzann reminded Holly to answer the questions she'd been asking in her letters. She still needed a good definition of "prayer warrior."

Suzann also phoned Mike, giving him a good tongue-lashing. She didn't regret a bit of it.

"I've been in Spain," he'd said, "resting."

Resting, my foot, she thought. Mike was probably with that little blonde he was seeing before he left for Texas.

He promised to take Holly's phone calls now and escort her around Hollywood. Sensing his true attitude regarding her sister, however, Suzann half wished she'd fired him on the spot.

She'd located a Bible on Holly's bookcase. Still feeling itchy, she gathered the Bible and her Sunday School teacher's manual, carrying both to the couch for further study.

On Sunday morning, Suzann emerged from her car, ready to tackle both her classes. She'd carefully hidden most of her pink spots behind a long-sleeved, rust-colored dress that she found in Holly's closet. Still, sometimes her bites itched terribly.

Mrs. Beesley caught up to Suzann before she reached her Sunday School classroom. Breathlessly, the older woman informed her that her nephew from Dallas planned to visit her shortly, perhaps on the coming weekend.

"I told him all about you, Miss Harmon," Mrs. Beesley said, "and he's anxious to meet you."

"Oh...how nice," Suzann said vaguely. "Will he be doing any preaching while he's here?"

"I hope so. But Pastor Jones hasn't said one way or the other yet."

Suzann ended the conversation with a tired smile. She simply had to get to bed earlier. Living Holly's ordinary life was exhausting. With a determined air of enthusiasm, she entered the building where her class waited.

Her adult class went well. So did Suzann's first session with her Vacation Bible School class the next morning.

The children appeared to enjoy having something to do during the first week of their two-week fall vacation. Their excitement spilled over, causing Suzann to think about the holidays ahead.

At first she'd discouraged Holly from telling her parents about the switch. But pretending that she was the Harmons's daughter would have been hard to pull off. Now that they knew, she wouldn't have to spend Thanksgiving or Christmas with them.

Suzann eluded Josh until snack time.

As the children ate their snow cones, she saw him looking at her. She wasn't surprised when he finally cornered her at the water fountain.

"I just learned that my unpaid assistant that helps out with my youth ministry is out of town and will be gone at least two weeks." His blue eyes bubbled with an undercurrent of mischief. "Are you available to fill in until she returns?"

She knew she should say no. She also knew that Holly *would* want to do something like this.

"What would you want me to do?"

"Just ride along in the church van with me and the kids whenever we go somewhere."

"Will we be the only sponsors?"

"Sometimes," he said. "But most of the time, we can count on at least one parent-volunteer."

"That's encouraging." She cast her eyes upward—toward Heaven. *I can't believe I'm doing this,* she thought. She hesitated, shaking her head from side to side. "So, when would I start?"

Jollity danced from the depths of his gaze. "We're planning a skating trip to San Antonio, but I don't know when yet. I'll let you know."

"Okay," she said reluctantly, "we'll leave it this way—if you can't find anyone else, I'll go to San Antonio as one of the sponsors."

"Fair enough."

Somehow she knew that there wouldn't be another volunteer. She was the youth group's unpaid sponsor, at least for the next two weeks.

Just as she turned to go back inside, Josh displayed that boyish grin of his again. She'd never met a man quite like him. Charming, yet wholesome and honest. She also loved his sense of humor.

Josh Gallagher would be a tough act for any man to follow.

Shortly before eight on Friday night, Suzann sat in Holly's tiny living room, waiting for the TV movie she'd selected to flash on the screen. The announcer came on instead.

"*Forever Darling* won't be showing tonight after

all," he said. "Instead, we are privileged to show you *Lovenest*, starring Suzann Condry and Greer Fraser."

Rats. Suzann aimed the remote at the screen and clicked.

She was beginning to recover from her ordeal, to settle down slightly. The last thing she needed was to see all those old love scenes again. She and Greer had filmed that movie in Spain. No wonder she begrudged Mike his recent trip there.

She'd just picked up a book and started reading when the phone rang. She put down her book and lifted the receiver to her ear.

"Hello."

"Hi," Kate said. "How does it feel to have Vacation Bible School behind you?"

"Great. You're lucky your job kept you from helping."

"Isn't that the truth?" Kate laughed. "And how are your chiggers bites? Is the medicine still working?"

"Like a charm." Suzann paused contemplatively. "Who told you about my chigger bites? Josh Gallagher?"

"Who else?"

Suzann wondered why Kate and the assistant pastor were obviously so close, but decided not to ask. After all, Kate had said they grew up together and had always been good friends. It wasn't surprising that they would chat once in a while.

"Small town life never ceases to amaze me," Suzann said.

"When have you lived anywhere else?"

She'd made another mistake. Why did she always mess up in front of Kate Devlon?

"Just because I was raised on a ranch, miles from the nearest small town, doesn't mean I haven't wished for something different."

"Maybe your real calling is the movies," Kate said.

"Where would you get an idea like that?"

"Just kidding. But that reminds me of the real reason I called."

"I can hardly wait to hear."

"Then why don't you turn on your TV to channel eight and see for yourself?"

Suzann felt her body go rigid. "What's on channel eight?"

"Remember how you always said you had a twin sister, somewhere?"

"Yes."

"I think I might have found her on channel eight."

"What are you talking about?" Suzann swallowed nervously.

"You look a lot like Suzann Condry, Holly. Honest. Everyone thinks so."

"Give me a break."

"Don't take my word," Kate said. "Turn on the TV and see for yourself."

The next morning at Holly's dressing table, Suzann's thoughts centered on the telephone conversation she'd had with Kate Devlon on the previous night. Did Kate suspect something? She was frighteningly close to the truth regarding Suzann's identity.

If Kate could figure things out so easily, it would only be a matter of time before others in the community arrived at that same conclusion—unless Suzann came up with a plan to throw them off her path.

Suzann reached for her brush, gripping it firmly as she brushed her hair. In the future she would admit the obvious. She resembled Suzann Condry. Denying the similarity could draw unwanted attention, destroy this "normal" life she'd borrowed.

Life as a member of Oak Valley Bible Church could hardly be called normal. But at least it was different from the life she'd known prior to coming here. That counted for something.

Suzann peered in the old-fashioned oval mirror. She hardly recognized her reflection. Would she ever get used to wearing glasses? She adjusted the black plastic frames for perhaps the tenth time that morning. If she hoped to keep Holly's job at Oak Valley Bible Church, she would need to pour more of herself into her Holly Harmon character.

Suzann reminded herself that the youth of the church were going on a skating trip to San Antonio that morning. She'd promised Josh that she'd help out as a substitute sponsor.

For two cents, Suzann would call Josh and say she was ill again and unable to travel. Being with Josh all day was *not* a smart idea. On the other hand, if she backed out, who would go in her place? She wouldn't allow the children to miss their outing on her account.

Suzann continued to brush her hair with long even

strokes. The rhythmic movement felt familiar, sooth-
ing. Forty-eight, forty-nine, fifty times exactly.

She reached into the jewelry box for Holly's pearl
earrings, wondering how her sister was handling the
heavy makeup that a California movie star applied
every morning.

Something gold fell out of the box, spinning off
the dressing table. She knew intuitively that it was the
locket her mother had given her shortly before she
died.

Down on all fours, Suzann spread out her fingers
in search of the heart-shaped object. The blue carpet
felt woolly and smooth under her hands. Reaching
out, her long fingers touched cold metal, then a dainty
chain. A flood of memories clutched her internally
with an excruciating sting.

Suzann had worn the locket to the cabin the day
she arrived in Texas so that Holly could see the tiny
pictures inside of the couple who had adopted her.
She'd also worn it to her mother's funeral, but she
hadn't worn it in Oak Valley.

On hearing the news that her mother had died, Suzann's throat had contracted, and she'd had a difficult
time breathing. It had hurt that she hadn't had time
to say good-bye.

After the funeral, when Suzann was going through
her mother's things, she'd found a copy of her birth
certificate that she had never seen before, stating that
she was adopted. Was that what her mother had
planned to tell her on the day she died? Now she
would never know.

Why had her mother delayed telling her that she

was adopted until it was too late? And why had the adoption agency allowed twins to be separated? She'd always thought there was a rule against that.

She put the necklace and all the memories that went with it back in her sister's jewelry box. If she expected to be on time for the skating trip, she would need to finish dressing.

Suzann blinked, recalling once more the movie starring Suzann Condry that Kate had mentioned. She wondered if anyone she'd see today had watched channel eight the previous night. Were her days as Holly Harmon already numbered?

Chapter Five

Suzann was standing at the living room window, looking out, when Josh arrived. She watched him park the church van on the side street adjacent to her apartment house. Then she stepped out onto the porch, preferring to join him there rather than inviting him inside.

In jeans and a blue print blouse, she felt very much the Texas girl she claimed to be. She'd managed to push back most of those troubling thoughts that were hounding her, but Josh stuck in her mind like glue.

Descending the flight of stairs two at a time, she promised herself three things. She wouldn't encourage Josh anymore. She wouldn't accept anymore of his invitations. And if he suggested one more time that she spend Thanksgiving with him at his family's hill country ranch, she would plug up her ears.

Sure, he appeared to like her. However, Suzann was convinced that people seldom said what they really meant or felt.

Let's face it. Josh Gallagher couldn't be as great as Kate said he was. Nobody could. She was right to keep him at arm's length.

About a dozen noisy children had crowded into the van. Josh had picked the children up first, meaning that she and Josh wouldn't be alone for a minute. Robby Sullivan sat by an open window, waving to her and smiling from ear to ear.

"I see Robby's here," she said to Josh.

He nodded and grinned. "And the Howard brothers."

"This is sure to be an interesting day."

"Day?" His grin deepened. "I wish."

"What are you saying?"

Josh opened the van door for Suzann on the passenger side. "I won't be driving this crew back to Oak Valley until way after dark."

"Is there anything else you failed to mention?"

"Maybe you should get in first."

Josh would be driving the van. Suzann sat next to the door, leaving a large space between them. Gazing behind her, she counted ten children, four boys and six girls.

Ben and Glen Howard waved. "Hi, Miss Harmon."

Suzann smiled, waving back. Then she faced the street ahead again. "Okay, Brother Josh, what is it you forgot to tell me?"

He laughed and started the motor. "Mrs. Beesley and her nephew, Dexter Simpson, are our other two sponsors."

"How did that happen?"

"Brother and Sister Winslow backed out at the last minute. And as you know, my regular volunteer is out of town."

"Lovely."

Suzann could only imagine what someone with a name like Dexter might be like. She'd always associated the name with Dexter Quin, the meanest child actor she had ever met.

She glanced back again. There was hardly room for one more person, much less two.

"Will Mrs. Beesley and her nephew be meeting us in San Antonio?" she asked.

"No. I'm on my way to pick them up right now." Josh stopped at a stop sign. His eyes twinkled playfully when they united with Suzann's. "Mrs. Beesley lives about ten miles out of town on the road that Ts into the San Antonio highway."

Suzann nodded, trying not to show her displeasure. She still liked Mrs. Beesley. However, an all-day dose of aunt and nephew together might be more than she could take. When Josh's mocking smile slammed against her guilty conscience, she knew her disapproval had surfaced.

"There's something else I forgot to tell you," he said.

"Let's have it."

"I just found out that my full-time volunteer-assistant, Milly Parker, is *moving* to Kansas next week—not just visiting there. She's there now, looking for an apartment."

"So?"

"I need someone to take her place." He studied Suzann imploringly.

"No way, José."

Josh responded with one of his heart-stopping smiles, then turned his gaze back to the road.

"But you're so great with children, and they all like you." He glanced toward the back of the van. "Isn't that right, kids?" He nodded as if he wanted them to follow suit. "Say yes."

"Yes!" the children chorused.

"See?" Josh shrugged. "What more can I say? So will you take the job, Miss Harmon?"

"*N-O.*" She shook her head. "In case you didn't know, that spells *no.*"

"I can agree that the pay stinks," he went on. "In fact, all you'll get are free meals and free tickets when we go somewhere. But I can promise you some great Saturdays in San Antonio and the surrounding area."

Suzann squinted at Josh doubtfully.

"It's not too late to accept," Josh said.

Suzann shook her head.

He gestured to the children with his left hand, briefly, like a band director beckoning the brass section to increase the volume.

"Say yes, Miss Harmon!" the children cried out together. "Say yes!"

Suzann frowned. "Why do I get the feeling you guys rehearsed all this before I got in the van?"

"Why, Miss Harmon," Josh said with an innocent look, "I'm surprised at you. Surely you don't think we would stoop so low."

"I certainly do think so. But I'm not buying."

"I think you should be honored that the children like you so much. They'll be crushed if you refuse."

Suzann noted Josh's beseeching expression and looked toward the back again. "Well, this is really an honor, kids. Thanks a lot, and I'd really like to say yes but..."

"Please, Miss Harmon," one of the little girls said. "We need you."

Need. Many had said Suzann was beautiful and talented. Nobody had ever said they needed her, until that instant. It silenced her just hearing the word for the first time. It also got her to thinking.

Holly would probably have agreed to become Josh's unpaid assistant no matter what. Suzann was supposed to be Holly. Just because accepting the job meant she would be spending more time with Josh didn't mean they would be alone together. She'd see to that.

Why, how could they be alone with ten screaming children around all the time? And they were *sweet,* screaming children.

"Will you do it, Miss Harmon?" Robby asked. "*Pretty* please."

"Oh, all right," she said without enthusiasm. "I guess I will."

The children raised their hands and shouted. "Yeaaaaa!"

Josh smiled down at Suzann. "Ditto."

Ignoring him, Suzann added, "But I'm warning you, gang. You better behave, or I'm out of here. Okay?"

The children shouted again. "Okay!"

Ben Howard gave his younger brother another give-me-five slap on his open palm to seal the deal.

Josh slowed the van, pointing toward a rock cottage in the shadow of a pecan grove. "Mrs. Beesley lives there."

Suzann thought the house looked as warm and cosy and as full of secrets as Mrs. Henrietta Beesley herself.

A tall man in his early thirties with dark hair escorted Mrs. Beesley to the church van. The chatty little woman introduced her nephew. Then she reminded Suzann that Dexter had been counting the days until he could meet Miss Harmon.

Dexter Simpson sent Suzann a pleading grin tinged with embarrassment. It was a friendly smile, she noticed, in spite of the circumstances that provoked it.

"Now, Dexter," Mrs. Beesley said, "I insisted that you sit up front with the young folks. I'll just sit here in the back with the children."

Dexter shrugged and opened the door on Suzann's side. She scooted over in order to make room for him.

Mrs. Beesley's nephew was downright handsome. So why did he need his Aunt Henrietta to find him a girlfriend? If Suzann's instincts were right, he didn't. A man like Dexter Simpson probably had Christian women all over Dallas swooning over him.

Why if it weren't for his uninspiring name, he would be perfect for— For Kate Devlon, of course. Suzann laughed at herself mentally for sounding so much like a matchmaker. If she weren't so busy all the time, she'd attribute her romantic tendencies to the fact that she didn't have enough to do.

"Will you be preaching in church tomorrow?" Suzann asked Dexter. "Your aunt said that you might."

"No," he said, "I won't be doing any preaching. But I will be giving my testimony."

Testimony, Suzann thought. She knew what the word meant in regard to court cases. Still, she should remember to ask Holly what Christians meant by that particular word.

Suzann was still trying to fully understand what Christians meant by *prayer warriors.* She'd been studying the concept diligently, but she still hadn't done any actual praying. She was about to bring up that very subject when Josh leaned forward, then glanced right at Dexter Simpson.

"I'm looking forward to hearing your testimony in church in the morning. I understand you just returned from a missionary trip to Mexico."

"That's true," Dexter said. "A group from our church was there almost six weeks. Unfortunately, I was only able to be there for two."

"What's Mexico like right now?" Josh asked.

"The people are open to the gospel, I think. But many in the country are poor and needy. There's still work to do there."

"Amen to that," Josh said.

A road sign read 25 miles to San Antonio. A billboard farther down read Iceland Skating.

Josh turned to Suzann. "I'm not much of a skater. How about you, Miss Harmon?"

"Frankly, I haven't been on a pair of roller skates since I was a child."

"Roller skates? I thought you knew we were going to an ice-skating rink."

"Now you're talking," Suzann said. "Ice skating, I can do."

Would a Texas native like Holly know how to ice skate? She knew Holly had never lived in a city as large as San Antonio where ice skating rinks were available. She hated lying now, but it appeared to be the only option she had.

"We were visiting friends in Houston one summer," Suzann added, "and the kids went ice skating almost every day, just to cool off. I learned to skate then."

"Dexter grew up in Houston," Mrs. Beesley explained from the back seat. "Did I mention that?"

Suzann nodded slowly. "Yes, I believe you did."

Mrs. Beesley chattered on for several minutes, drowning out most of the children. Suzann tried to overlook the comical expressions Josh sent her.

All at once Robby Sullivan stood and leaned his head over the front seat. "Brother Josh has a girlfriend," he said in a singsong voice. "Brother Josh has a—"

"Enough." Suzann turned, sending Robby a "shushing" gesture.

Dexter leaned over, peering at Josh. "I hadn't realized that you and Miss Harmon were...."

"We're not," Suzann inserted. "Robby and his friends have a huge imagination."

Josh's forehead wrinkled. "Sit down, Robby, and behave yourself."

The air at the skating rink felt frosty and fresh. The climate between Josh and Suzann was even colder than that. Suzann was about to roll out and join the others when Dexter appeared at her side.

"Would you like to skate doubles?" he asked.

The ice looked smooth and inviting. She wanted to say yes. It had been ages since she skated with a partner, and she had a hunch Dexter would be an excellent skater. But Josh seemed upset about something. Perhaps he felt she wasn't helping enough with the children. She didn't want to make matters worse.

"I can't," Suzann said. "I can barely keep from falling as a single."

"Maybe another time?"

"Maybe." Suzann motioned toward Mrs. Beesley. "Why not ask your aunt instead?"

"She didn't bother to rent a pair of skates," Dexter said. "You don't mind if I skate along beside you, do you?"

"Of course not."

After helping the children put on skates and get out on the ice, Suzann and Dexter sat side by side, watching the skaters. Josh studied the rink from a folding chair five empty seats away, with Mrs. Beesley directly to his left. Dexter's aunt appeared to be keeping Josh entertained, talking endlessly. Still, Josh found time to gaze at Suzann from time to time.

"With that Sunday job of mine," Dexter said, "I don't get down to Oak Valley very often. But I hope I'll see you, Miss Harmon, the next time I do make it down."

"I'm looking forward to it."

Dexter shared some interesting facts about the Bible. She told him about her friend, Kate Devlon. Finally she said, "I'm also interested in learning more about prayer warriors."

"Prayer warriors," Dexter repeated. "Now there's an interesting topic. The entire subject of spiritual warfare is probably a mystery to everyone outside the church."

Spiritual warfare? Another term to add to her I-don't-know list, no doubt.

"I'd like to read more on the subject," Suzann said. "Can you suggest a book?"

"I could suggest several. But let me send you a sermon I wrote for our church recently on just that subject. It explains more than I could possibly tell now."

"Thank you—Dex. I'd really like to read your sermon."

She wrote down her mailing address on the back of an old skating rink program Dexter found. Josh frowned, she noticed, when she handed the program back to Dexter.

After supper, they headed back to the van.

Suzann had hoped to find a seat in the back. But by the time she got there, Mrs. Beesley had already squeezed her way between the Howard brothers. Suzann had no choice but to sit in the front seat between Josh and Dexter Simpson again.

All day she'd tried to avoid contact with Josh Gallagher, and she had failed miserably. It looked as though the drive home would be long and trying.

* * *

Holly draped the delicate dress across the big, four-poster bed in the master bedroom. The dress had arrived late that Saturday afternoon from the designer. Running the palm of her right hand across the beaded bodice, Holly took in every detail. She'd never seen a garment as fine and expensive as this one—except on TV when they televised the Academy Awards ceremony.

It was an original from an exclusive designer, made of soft, satiny material the color of polished silver. From the look of it, the dress must have cost thousands of dollars. Why, the beads alone looked like real diamonds. She wondered if they were.

The neckline was cut in a V in front, but not too low. She could be thankful to her sister for that. The circular skirt was made of yards and yards of material. She imagined herself wearing the dress, mentally heard the *whoosh* it might make when she moved.

The shoes were silver too, another famous, high-fashion designer. She would be carrying a matching silver clutch purse with the same beaded design.

Holly had wanted Suzann to be saved, and she still did. Yet when she looked at clothes as fine as this, she wondered if one of the reasons she agreed to the switch was to experience a whole new world that she might never otherwise have known.

If her twin sister wasn't her fairy godmother, she was a close second. Everything would be perfect if she were going to the premiere with Shawn instead of his older brother.

Holly unhooked the dress from its hanger and slipped it over her head. The smooth feel of the material brushed her body softly, flowing downward to the floor. Reaching around with her left hand, she sucked in her breath and zipped up the back.

She felt as if she'd been poured into it. Standing in front of the full-length mirror, she realized that she looked that way too. She would need to lose a few pounds before she wore it outside the master bedroom.

Satin and diamonds were eons from the jeans and cowboy boots Holly was accustomed to wearing. What else would one wear on a remote ranch in west Texas?

If her mother wanted to buy so much as a loaf of bread, she had to drive at least seventy-five miles. The family traveled even farther on Sunday morning when they drove into El Paso to attend church.

It wasn't surprising that as children and teenagers, Holly and her younger brothers were shy around strangers. However, they were quite skilled in making their thoughts and wishes known. Their father made sure of that.

Christian values were taught around the supper table. Each family member was allowed to express an opinion on a variety of issues. The only request her father made was that Holly and her brothers back up their views with scripture verses.

Holly took off the satin dress, draping it over a coat hanger.

"Miss Condry," the housekeeper called from the other side of the bedroom door. "You have a guest waiting downstairs—Mr. McDowell."

"Which one?"

"Mr. Mike McDowell, ma'am."

Holly's forehead wrinkled. "Tell him I'll be right down."

She changed into a pair of expensive-looking navy slacks, made of a drapy fabric, a gold-colored silk blouse, and navy pumps. Her outfit looked perfect for a movie star. What would Mike say if she showed up in jeans, tennis shoes and a T-shirt?

Glamour and sophistication. Suzann had said that temporarily, those must be Holly's goals. Holly buttoned the top pearl button of her blouse as she glided down the winding stairway.

Halfway down, she noticed Mike. He stood in the archway separating the entry hall from the blue sitting room, looking as cocky and self-assured as ever.

"How was Spain?" she asked with a trace of sarcasm.

"Great. And how have you been?"

"Do you really care?"

He put his forefinger over his lips, shushing her. "We can talk in the Blue Room," he said.

"We can talk on the patio because that's where I'm going. Care to join me?"

"What happened to the sweet, little Christian girl I met at the cabin?" he asked. "Don't tell me she's gone Hollywood."

Ignoring him, she moved down the hall in the direction of the back door. On her way out, Holly stuck her head in the formal dining room.

Gertie was dusting a chair. The question was, why? It was almost 7:00 p.m., California time. Gertie's household chores should have been over hours ago.

The strong scent of furniture polish mingled with the woodsy fragrance of air freshener. Holly's eyes watered. She was afraid she might sneeze.

"Gertie, would you mind sending lemonade and some of those little sandwiches you make out to the patio later." Holly smiled supportively. "I'll be visiting with Mr. McDowell there. Oh, and you also might want to open a window when you're applying that lemon wax."

"Yes, ma'am. Oh, and another thing—I won't be here in the morning. I have to take Buddy in for a doctor appointment. That's why I'm doing my morning chores now."

"That's just fine, Gertie."

The patio provided seclusion while furnishing them with a panoramic view of the flower garden and the lighted pool. She took a chair at the heavy, iron table and motioned for Mike to join her.

"You're managing to pull this off," he said. "Congratulations. If I didn't know better, I'd swear you really were Suzann Condry."

"You've been out of the country for days. What makes you think I'm not?"

Her implications appeared to startle him. Then he smiled. "You really had me going there." He chuckled softly. "You're good. Really good. Did you know that?"

"I'm Suzann Condry. I'm supposed to be good."

"I like the way you're playing this out."

"Speaking of playing, you still haven't told me about your trip to Spain."

"Later. I want to hear what you've been up to while I was away."

"Then I would suggest you ask your brother."

"Good shot." He hesitated. "I'll say this. You sure don't sound like the mousy little librarian I met in Texas."

Mousy. She wasn't surprised. She already knew that's what he thought of her. Besides, Mike's opinion didn't matter much to her anymore.

She tried to smile. "I'm glad you approve of my disguise."

"You're perfect—in more ways than one."

He reached across the table and attempted to take her hand in his. Holly pretended not to notice and waved to Gertie, coming toward them with a tray of food and two frosty glasses.

Gertie put the tray on the table.

"Everything looks great, Gertie. Thanks." Holly glanced up at the housekeeper and smiled. "I believe that will be all."

Mike didn't speak again until Gertie had gone back inside.

"You sure have her fooled," he said, "and that's a plus. The family and the household staff are always the hardest to deceive."

"What about directors, actors Suzann has worked with, and former boyfriends? Will Greer Fraser be easy to dupe?"

"I've spread the word around that you're ill. So you won't have to see anyone until you recover."

"Am I terminal?" Holly asked.

"Not really." He laughed. "Just a light case of walking pneumonia."

"In that case, maybe I'll be able to attend the premiere and wear that fancy dress of Suzann's after all. I'd hate to be hospitalized before I've had the chance to really see California."

This time his laugh came from deep within him. "I like you, Holly Harmon."

Unfortunately, she thought, I don't feel the same about you.

"And I know someone like you will understand what I'm about to say," he continued.

Here it comes, she thought.

"Something else came up," Mike said. "I'll be unable to take you to the opening after all. Shawn promised to go in my place. Can you handle that?"

Thank you, Jesus.

Holly wanted to shout her thanks in a hundred languages. She might have, if she'd known a hundred languages.

"As long as my sister knows, I'm sure something can be worked out."

Mike looked surprised. "You want to tell Suzann about this?"

"I'm afraid that's the only way I'll agree to it."

Chapter Six

Suzann hummed along as the sound of the children singing filled the van that night. Seated between Josh and Dexter, she kept reviewing her situation, reflecting on a new and different problem that was beginning to concern her.

Earlier that evening, Mrs. Beesley told her how a young girl had recovered from a near-fatal illness after some people in her church prayed for her. And she'd called those who prayed for the girl "prayer warriors."

Two months ago Suzann would have called such a story hogwash, or the ravings of a group of Christian nuts. Now she thought Mrs. Beesley's account sounded almost believable.

Was she becoming one of them? The mere thought overwhelmed her. She rubbed her forehead with the palm of her right hand.

At first, she'd rationalized. She was simply consumed by her new identity as Holly Harmon and was just overplaying her role. Nothing to worry about.

Now she knew she was losing her perspective, along with her charm and sophistication. Was she also losing her grip?

At some level, she sounded more like Pollyanna than mild-mannered Holly Harmon. She bit her lower lip. Were these new convictions coming from a true change of heart? Or were they tempered by her feelings for Josh Gallagher?

Maybe she should consider visiting a good shrink. She could explain about her mother's recent death and....

No, she couldn't explain any of those things without revealing more than she wanted anyone to know. She thought of Pastor Jones's kind, gentle face as he stood behind the pulpit every Sunday morning.

Though Suzann had never had time to say more to Pastor Jones than an occasional ''hi'' when they passed in the hall, she knew instinctively that he was a man she could trust. His sermons proved that.

However, if she told Pastor Jones everything she wanted to tell, Holly could lose her job. She would just have to work things out alone.

Alone. According to Holly, Christians were never alone.

''The Lord is just a prayer away'' she'd said.

What a consoling thought. If only it were true.

Suzann squirmed in her seat, then steepled her hands, folding and unfolding them unconsciously. She knew Josh was upset about something. But there was nothing she could do about it.

As she'd expected, Josh returned Dexter and his aunt to the little rock house on their way back to Oak Valley. Next, he drove by the homes of the children and left them with their parents.

Finally, only Suzann and Josh remained in the church van.

At Suzann's apartment house, Josh got out of the van without saying a word. He went around to the passenger side and opened the door for Suzann.

Suzann would have to cut across the dark, side yard in order to reach the stairway leading to her upstairs apartment. It wasn't surprising that someone like Josh Gallagher wouldn't want her to find her way alone, insisting instead that he walk her to her door.

When she didn't argue, she expected a grin to reappear on Josh's face. He didn't smile, but he helped her out of the van.

The air outside felt cooler than when they had started back to Oak Valley. Downright cold in fact. A chilling wind rustled the trees outside. Suzann hadn't brought a coat.

The wind roared, lashing through her thin, blue cotton blouse. She lifted her shoulders and crossed her arms, hugging her chest and shivering. Her long hair blew in all directions. The heels of her tennis shoes crunched on the brownish carpet of grass.

"Looks like a norther just blew in," Josh said. "Could turn real cold tonight. Might rain, and we could sure use it."

Leave it to Josh Gallagher to lead with a weather report.

He put his arm protectively around Suzann's shoulders. "Cold?"

"A little."

A sweet warmth filled her chilled body. Suzann trembled. The cozy feeling went beyond the physical, digging deep into the emotional center of her being.

"That rain we got when you first came back from your vacation didn't go far enough," he continued, "but the weatherman never mentioned a word about a weather change. Let me get you inside before you get sick again."

They hurried up the stairs to the shelter of the front porch. Josh put his hands on her shoulders and turned her face toward his. "May I have your key?"

For an instant, his question stunned her because it held strong implications in California. Then Suzann relaxed, assured in the knowledge that Josh's intentions were honorable.

Nevertheless...

She smelled rain. A droplet dampened the tip of her upturned nose. Now they would have to go inside.

Suzann looked down, groping in her purse for her key. When she looked up, he finally smiled. With a deep sigh, she handed him the key.

Josh followed her inside and closed the door behind him.

"Why did you tell Brother Simpson that we weren't dating?" he demanded.

She hesitated, hoping to come up with an answer. "Well—" she pushed her hair back from her face "—we only went out to lunch once when we worked at the bake sale together. I'd hardly call that dating."

"I would." He put his hands on her cheeks. Holding her in place, he studied her lips with a tenderness that seemed to flow out of those blue eyes of his. "I hope to go out with you very soon."

Not if I have anything to say about it, she thought.

Josh lowered his head. Surely he didn't intend to kiss her. And why did she keep hoping he would?

Her eyes closed, just in case.

His warm lips brushed hers like the wings of a butterfly in midflight. Yet the kiss was over before it really began—soft and smooth and…and wonderful. She wanted the butterfly to come right back.

Had he really kissed her at all? Or had she only experienced a beautiful dream?

The dream continued suddenly. She felt his lips on hers again. The kiss deepened. She moved closer to him, waiting for another kiss.

He released her. Yet his gaze still focused on her mouth.

"I want to kiss you again. But I won't," he said firmly. He took a step back, increasing the space between them.

A wave of embarrassment swept over her. Suzann moved back too, pressing her body against the cold, white plaster wall behind her.

According to the rules her mother had taught her, the *female* was supposed to suggest that they stop before things went too far. Not her male counterpart. What must Josh think of her? What would Holly think if she knew?

"You wouldn't happen to have any coffee, would you?" he asked. "'Cause I could sure use a cup."

"Oh. Oh, sure," she said, snapping back to reality. "I'll go get some—some coffee right away." She waved both hands nervously toward the couch. "You, just sit. Right over there."

She practically flew into the kitchen. Then she fluttered around in search of the coffeepot like a hummingbird looking for a sugar-water feeder. She opened the cabinet door over the microwave and noticed him out of the corner of her eye, watching her from the doorway.

Well, at least her nervous retreat to the kitchen was not unlike something Holly would do. Now if she could just remember where she put the coffeepot, she might be able to settle down.

Casually, Josh moved to the cabinet above the refrigerator, opened the cabinet door, and pulled out the coffeepot. "Where's the coffee?" he asked.

"Coffee?"

Her mind went blank. How could super-organized Suzann Condry have forgotten where she put something she used every morning? On second thought, was it any wonder that she was having a hard time focusing—with Josh standing there, smiling at her like that?

"What did you say?" she asked finally, stalling for time.

"I was asking where you keep the coffee," he said, "but I just remembered." Still grinning, he opened the pantry door by the stove. "Here we go."

She took the coffee can from him with trembly hands. "I'll do this." She cocked her head toward the living room door. "You—you just go back in there and relax."

He propped his elbow against the refrigerator door. The dash of humor in his gaze took on tender overtones. "If it's all the same to you, I'd rather stay and watch."

Okay, so she wasn't so great in the kitchen. There were a lot of other things she did very well. At the moment, however, she couldn't think of a single one.

Somehow, she managed to prepare a fair to middling pot of coffee and placed it on a tray with two china cups, the creamer and sugar bowl.

He followed her into the living room, settling beside her on the couch as she served the coffee. Did he intend to kiss her again? Or maybe head a discussion on why he should never have kissed her in the first place?

Holding the handle of her steaming cup with her right hand, she tried to regain some shred of composure, to save her sanity if for no other reason. Dare she bring up her reaction to his kisses?

Or perhaps they should have an in-depth discussion of the weather. That subject was sure to interest Josh. She smiled inwardly.

"Good coffee," he remarked.

"If I can make decent coffee, anyone can."

His lighthearted chuckle set her at ease. "We need to start practicing that duet we've been putting off for so long," he said. "Pastor Jones is beginning to think we never intend to do the song."

"All right, we can do that."

"The children's Christmas program is coming up," he added, "and we need a director."

"Oh no, you don't. You're not talking me into *that*."

With shaky fingers Suzann set her cup and saucer on the coffee table in front of them. The cup rattled against the saucer. Hot coffee sloshed over the side of the cup.

Josh didn't appear to notice. "Then who would you suggest I ask?" he demanded. "Mrs. Beesley?"

"Oh, well, Mrs. Beesley is certainly not a good choice," Suzann said. "With her aching back and all. I'm sure we can come up with someone more suitable."

"Any suggestions?"

"Now don't hurry me. I'm trying to think." She waited meditatively. "What about Kate? She's young enough to handle the strain, and the last I heard, she has no back problems at all."

"No experience," he said flatly. "You're the only one who's had any real experience with something like this."

If you only knew, she thought.

"What about Robby's mother?" Suzann said. "She's in the choir this year."

"True, but she wasn't in the Christmas program last year. You were. And you were also in the choir."

"I'm not a director."

"Everyone thinks you'd be perfect for the job."

"Who's everybody?"

He counted with his fingers. "Well, there's me and—and—" a mischievous grin appeared, and he touched his second finger "—then there's me, of course, and there's—"

"You." She laughed softly. "I think I get the picture."

He held up all ten fingers. "With all these people rooting for you, how can you refuse?"

Suzann shook her head. "Josh Gallagher, you're impossible."

"Impossible?" He eyed her lips again.

Her smile faded.

"Nothing's impossible," he said. "You just have to go after what you think God wants for your life."

Suddenly she realized that they weren't talking about choirs or Christmas pageants.

Suzann got up early the next morning to attend Sunday School and church. A chill filled her slender body as she stepped out onto the wooden porch. The north wind whipped her brown leather jacket, flattening her tan wool skirt against long legs. Turning her face toward the wind, she raced to her car.

From the choir loft later, she listened intently as Dexter Simpson gave his testimony. She learned not only a little more about Dexter, but what Christians meant by their "testimony."

Dexter began by describing how he "found the Lord." The term still puzzled Suzann, reminding her of a missing person who had suddenly been located. As Dexter explained it, that was exactly what happened. Totally immersed in what he was saying, she leaned forward in her pew in hopes of hearing more.

Dexter said that he'd wandered aimlessly through

life with no clear destination other than the career his father had chosen for him. He was expected to take over his father's insurance business and make more money than his father had made.

Making a lot of money had seemed like a worthy goal. But was it right for Dexter? In the end, he'd decided it wasn't.

For Suzann, hearing Dexter's testimony was like hearing a replay of her own life. She'd wandered too, fulfilling her mother's dream by becoming an actress and model without a focus of her own. Even now, she had no clear aspirations.

Apparently Dexter had chosen the easy way out. First, he declared his belief in God. Then he merely proclaimed all the unsatisfactory things in life as good, and went on from there.

"All things work together for good," Dexter had quoted from Scripture, "for those that love the Lord."

Yet Suzann knew only too well that there were no easy answers.

After the Sunday service that night, Suzann met Josh in the choir room to practice their duet. She assumed they would both be singing a modern arrangement of "Amazing Grace." It never occurred to her that he was only to accompany her on his steel guitar.

Josh ran nimble fingers across the strings of his electric guitar in a brief introduction that seemed to set the mood. Suzann had no idea how Holly would have interpreted the music. Somehow, it didn't matter. The words and music had captured her completely.

She trembled with emotion, the music stirring her and speaking to her heart. It was as if the melody filled her being with a new understanding and a kind of wonder. Interpreting as she went along, she felt a tender kinship with the Divine Composer who inspired the hymn—as if, for an instant, she caught a glimpse of Him.

Swelling to an emotionally charged crescendo, Suzann pulled the mike from her face and dropped her arm.

"Amen," Josh said. "That was beautiful."

"Beautiful?" For an instant, she'd forgotten where she was.

"I know it isn't a Christmas song, but I want you to sing 'Amazing Grace' at the Christmas pageant next month."

"I thought *I* was the director."

"After hearing you, I think you might be the *show*."

"I don't think I should sing at all," she said. "The children are the show, and I have no wish to upstage them."

"A voice as sweet and pure as yours could never upstage anyone."

Pure? If only that were true.

Suzann went over to the open shelves by the piano in search of sheet music of some kind. Anything to keep from responding to what he'd just said.

He came over to the shelves as well and pulled out a booklet with a nativity scene on the cover. "Here. This copy is yours."

Suzann opened the songbook to the first page.

"The score looks difficult. Shouldn't we have started this project sooner?"

"The children have been singing the songs in the songbook in Sunday School for months," he said. "But we're really going to have to hit the practice sessions *hard* after Thanksgiving."

"I would think so." Suzann put the music booklet in her oversize handbag. "I'm bushed. I think I'll go on home."

"I'd offer you a ride," he said, "but..."

She nodded and pulled out her keys, dangling them in front of her. A soft tinkling sound destroyed the sudden silence that had enveloped them.

"At least I can walk you to your car," he said.

"That's not necessary, really."

"Yes, it is. It's dark out. Besides, I'm going that way anyway."

"Oh?"

"I parked right next to you."

Suzann nodded, and they headed for the parking lot. She felt suddenly exhausted by the effort of keeping Josh at arm's length. If she continued to spend this much time with him, he'd soon have her heart. She was already starting to dream about Josh every night.

She was a fraud who planned to disappear—eventually. It didn't take a brain surgeon to know that a movie star with a past was a mismatched love interest for a man of faith like Josh Gallagher. And she still had five months to go before fulfilling her promise to her sister.

Chapter Seven

Holly shook hands with the pastor of Burbank Independent Bible Fellowship that same Sunday evening. Then she stood on the bottom step just outside the foyer of the church, waiting for Shawn to join her. He was already a member of the congregation. After hearing Pastor Paulson's sermon, Holly thought she might like to join too.

As she stood there in the glow of the security lights, all one hundred and ten pounds of her, she saw someone watching. A man with a camera. An instant later, she saw a flash.

The man moved forward, sticking a microphone in her face.

"Miss Condry," he said. "I'm a reporter for RQST TV in Los Angeles, and our audience would like to know. Are you a member of this church now or just visiting?"

"Visiting," she managed to say.

"We heard that you've been very ill, perhaps dying. But you seem in good physical shape right now. To what do you attribute your quick recovery? God?''

Holly hesitated, wishing she could throw that mike of his out of his hand and over the hedge by the parking lot. She hated lying, but he was making it impossible to do otherwise.

Was this what it was like to be in the public eye? No wonder her sister retreated to Oak Valley, Texas.

She was about to say, "No comment," when someone pushed her from behind.

"I'm so sorry, ma'am," a young man said.

Holly glanced back. A crowd had gathered behind her, all trying to leave the church, and she was blocking their way. When she stepped aside to let them through, Shawn grabbed her arm.

"Come on," he said. "Let's get out of here."

"That reporter recognized me," Holly whispered. "Or should I say, he recognized Suzann."

"I know." He opened the passenger door of his van. "Get in before he finds us again."

She saw another flash.

"I think he just did."

Holly put her black patent-leather clutch purse in front of her face. But it was already too late. The reporter flashed his camera again.

Shawn went around to the driver's side of the vehicle, got in, and gunned the motor. "Get in," he insisted.

She closed her eyes briefly and shook her head. "That was just awful."

"I know."

She got in the van.

"Welcome to Tinsel Town," he said.

"Is it always like this?"

"Always, if a motion picture star is around, that is."

"Well, all I did was go to church. They certainly can't find anything bad to say about that."

"Oh, but you're wrong," he said. "You may recall that your sister has always made it quite clear that she doesn't believe in God. They can and will make a big story out of this."

"You could have warned me."

"Would you have agreed to drop out of church for six whole months, even if I had?"

She shook her head. "I could never do that."

"Then what would have been the point, other than to ruin your day?"

"I guess you're right."

"Of course I'm right." His warm smile lifted her spirits. "Where would you like to have supper?"

She shrugged, hoping he'd make that decision. "Any place where photographers dare not tread, I guess."

"I thought you might say that. And I know a little old lady from Pasadena who cooks the best pot roast and potatoes in California."

"You mean we're going to Pasadena?"

"Actually, the little old lady is my mother," he said, "and she lives about three blocks north of here. She sold her house in Pasadena and will continue to live with me until she finds a place of her own." He wheeled toward the freeway. "We live on Treatt Street."

"Treatt Street? What a catchy name."

He nodded. "I think that's a good address too, for someone like my mother who loves to bake cakes and pies, don't you?"

Holly smiled. "Yes, I certainly do. But hey," she said, "we're headed south. I thought you said your mother only lives a few blocks *north* of the church."

"She does. But before we can go there, we have to lose our tail."

"You mean the reporter guy is following us?"

"You got it." He motioned behind. "Take a look for yourself."

Holly glanced back. Her smile became an animated laugh. "Say, this is really neat. Like in the movies. Can you drive a little faster?"

"For you," he said, "I'll go as fast as the law allows."

It was after eight before they pulled up to the two-story white house on Treatt Street. Holly had imagined a small white-haired lady, standing at the kitchen table, flattening pie dough with a rolling pin. What she found was an attractive, middle-aged woman in a royal blue, silk dress, pushing back a silver curl that escaped her short, breezy hairstyle.

Shawn introduced Holly to his mother as Suzann Condry.

"Oh, Miss Condry," Lucy McDowell said, "I'm so glad to meet you. I see all your pictures."

"I'm glad somebody does," Holly said off the top of her head. Why did I say that? she asked herself.

After an embarrassing silence, everybody laughed nervously.

"I'm starved," Shawn said. "When do we eat?"

"Is that all you ever think about?" Mrs. McDowell said with a teasing tone.

Shawn draped one arm around Holly's shoulders and grinned at his mother. "If not food, what *should* I be thinking about?"

Ignoring him, Mrs. McDowell led the way into the dining room. The kitchen door was open. The smell of roast cooking blended with the scent of fresh apple pies.

The dining room table was set with expensive sterling-silver flatware and white china. Outdoor lighting coming in through the French doors danced on sparkling cut-glass tumblers filled with ice water. Miniature mums in shades of yellow and gold were arranged in a copper bowl, centering the dark, oak dining table.

As soon as Shawn said the blessing, his mother turned to him and smiled. "By the way, I saw someone snap Miss Condry's picture on my way back to the choir room this evening."

"You were in church tonight?" Holly said.

"I was singing in the choir."

"My mom is a great singer as well as a great cook," Shawn said. "But if she doesn't do something, fast, she's about to burn the roast."

Mrs. McDowell threw up both hands. "Oh, my goodness. I forgot all about it. Please, excuse me."

The meal was delicious. After they finished eating,

they went out onto the covered porch to have their pie and coffee.

The air felt cool and fresh against Holly's soft skin.

"I don't know if we're ever going to have any winter this year," Mrs. McDowell said. "Here it is almost Thanksgiving, and it was sixty-six degrees this morning." She turned to Holly. "You are planning to have Thanksgiving dinner with us, aren't you?"

Her question caught Holly by surprise. Shawn hadn't invited her.

"Of course she's having Thanksgiving dinner with us," Shawn asserted. "She just doesn't know it yet."

"Mike will be here too, of course," Mrs. McDowell said, "and his friend Natasha."

"Natasha, huh." Shawn grinned reflectively. "Never heard of her. She must be a new one."

"Now, Shawn," his mother scolded. "I won't have you saying unkind things about your brother."

Shawn exchanged a knowing glance with Holly. "Okay, Mom, whatever you say."

Lucy McDowell glanced back at Holly. "Tell me about your work, Miss Condry."

"Work?" What would Mrs. McDowell think if she told her about her real job at the church library in Oak Valley, Texas? "Oh," Holly said, "you mean at the studio?"

"That and your modeling job. Everything. It's all so exciting to someone like me."

"Frankly," Holly said, "I think your job as a member of the church choir is exciting too. It's certainly worthwhile."

"I'm so glad to hear you say that," Mrs. McDowell said. "I guess I'd always thought that..."

Her voice trailed off. A deep blush colored her cheeks.

"Miss Condry attended church this morning as my guest, Mom."

"I know that," Mrs. McDowell said. She turned to Holly. "What did you think of the preaching?"

"I thought the message was right on target," Holly said. "Teenagers today need to hear that sex was designed by God for marriage only."

Mrs. McDowell leaned forward in her chair. "It's so good to hear you say something like that. I had no idea someone like you would feel—"

"Mom," Shawn said, "I'm out of coffee, and the pot's almost empty. Would you like me to go inside and fix another pot?"

"Sit still. I'll do it."

Shawn sent Holly an embarrassed grin as his mother went back inside. "I want to apologize for my mom. She has no idea who you really are, and she's a little nervous—entertaining a movie star for the first time and all."

"No apologies are necessary."

"Mom has probably read all the tabloid stories about Suzann's rather notorious life-style," he said. "But I think she likes you, Holly. And I mean *you*, not Suzann Condry."

"That's very flattering," Holly said. "But I've read those tabloid stories too, unfortunately."

"Is that the reason you agreed to switch identities with your sister?" he asked.

Holly nodded. "It's my dream and earnest prayer that Suzann will find the Lord, right there in Oak Valley."

"That's a worthy prayer, all right." Shawn sent her a long, searching look. "And giving up your own life—even for just a few months—to save your sister's is a very noble thing to do."

Holly shrugged off his compliment. "It was nothing. I'm sure any Christian in my shoes would have done the same thing."

"Some would," he said. "But I can think of plenty who wouldn't."

"You might be surprised to know that I had my doubts too about doing this, until I'd known my sister for almost a week. It's not easy for a Christian to live a lie."

"I've wondered about that," he said. "How do you manage to justify what you're doing?"

"I don't," Holly said. "I just put everything in God's hands, and leave the details to Him."

"Fair enough."

Mrs. McDowell hurried out of the house with a fresh pot of coffee. "Coffee, anyone?"

Holly covered the top of her cup with her left hand. "None for me, thanks."

Shawn held out his cup. "More for me, please. And thanks, Mom."

He'd pulled his chair closer to Holly's while his mother was inside. Without fanfare, he reached over and patted Holly's hand. Mrs. McDowell's eyes widened, and Holly knew she was worried about Shawn becoming involved with a woman like Suzann, whose many relationships were public knowledge.

Holly wished she could extinguish Mrs. McDowell's motherly concerns and tell her the truth. Instead, she offered Shawn's mother her coffee cup. "I think maybe I'd like another cup of coffee, after all."

Mrs. McDowell reached for the cup just as the telephone rang. "Excuse me." The older woman put down the coffeepot. Moving to the cellular telephone on the small, metal table by the door, she put the phone to her ear.

"Hello." There was a pause. "Story? No, I have nothing to say about Miss Condry." She hesitated again. "Please, don't—please don't call here again." She slammed down the phone.

Mrs. McDowell's face looked pinched. Her hands shook. Her eyes seethed with pent-up anger.

"A reporter?" Shawn asked.

"What else?" his mother said. "Those people are awful."

Holly tensed in her chair. Her sister had warned her about the press, but she hadn't expected to be followed so soon.

With Shawn's help, she'd escaped—this time. She wondered how long it would be before a reporter caught her alone somewhere.

"I'm so sorry to have caused you all this trouble, Mrs. McDowell," Holly said. "I should never have come here."

"Nonsense," Shawn said. "You have a perfect right to be here."

Before Holly could protest further, the phone rang again.

Shawn sprang to his feet. "Let me get it this time." He reached for the receiver. "Shawn McDowell here." He waited. Then he checked his watch. "I can be there in ten minutes."

"Who was that?" Mrs. McDowell asked as Shawn hung up the phone. "The hospital?"

Shawn nodded. "I need to be there right away." He sent Holly a look tinged with disappointment. "I'll call you a cab."

Holly knew Shawn was a doctor at Crystal-Bay Children's Hospital. Yet his call to duty caught her off guard.

"There's no need for you to waste time calling me a cab," she said. "You go on."

"Thanks for understanding."

As she walked him out to his car, she turned, glancing up at him. "Is the child seriously ill? The one you're going to the hospital to see, that is?"

"Yes." He looked away.

"I'll pray," Holly said. "Please tell the child's parents that I'll be praying."

He blinked. Then he nodded. "I'll tell them. You can count on it."

At ten that Sunday night, Shawn stopped by the mansion to see Holly. She felt concerned the moment she saw his tired, downcast expression, and it was all she could do to keep from reaching out to him as he stood in the doorway.

In the sitting room known as the Blue Room a few

minutes later, she asked, "How did it go at the hospital tonight?"

"Not good, I'm afraid." He sighed heavily. "The little boy I told you about—well, he died."

"Died? *Why?*"

"Money," he said sharply. "The parents are poor, and they didn't know I would have operated on him for free. They waited far too long before bringing him in for treatment."

Holly shook her head in disbelief. "This is terrible. What can we do to stop this from happening again?"

"We?" A brief grin surfaced. "Does this mean you'd like to help?"

"Of course I'd like to help. Just tell me what I can do, and I'll do it."

"I hope you mean that, because we've been hoping to find a celebrity to host a fund-raiser we've been planning. We intend to raise money to add a free wing to the hospital for poor kids with medical problems. We could also use a famous person to get on television and tell parents about our free services at Children's Hospital."

"I could do that," she said.

"What about the acting?"

"I'll wing it, if I have to."

"You know," he said, "you're incredible."

"No praises, please. I'm just doing what anyone would do in my shoes."

"Few Christians could fill your shoes as well as you do." Shawn lifted his coffee cup in a mock toast.

Holly sipped her coffee warily. Was she reading too much into all this attention Shawn was showering on her? After the way Mike had treated her, it was no wonder that Shawn felt sorry for her. By being kind, was he merely doing what any good Christian man would do under similar circumstances?

He'd changed out of the suit and tie he wore to church that night. Now in a blue dress shirt, he'd also put on a pair of brown cowboy boots.

Was he wearing boots to add inches to his height? In heels, she would be as tall as Shawn. Did he think something like that mattered to her? Had her Suzann Condry facade blinded him?

No, Shawn wasn't like that. She was imagining things. Still, for whatever reason, he appeared unable to see the real Holly Harmon or know how she really felt about him.

Compared to his flashy, overbearing brother, some women might not take notice of a man like Shawn. How wrong could they be? Holly had never met a gentler, more tender man than Shawn, nor had she ever seen a man who was more handsome.

She thought about him constantly. Yet he'd stayed at arm's length. He played the role of the big brother in Holly's life, her good friend, her protector, and he did that very well. But she wanted more. Were her feelings for Shawn too strong for her own good?

They were just starting on their second cup of coffee when Bates announced that a Mr. Roger Bairn was waiting to see her.

"Tell him to come in," Holly said.

Bates turned and left the Blue Room.

"Bairn," Shawn repeated. "Isn't he the private investigator your sister hired? I think I met him once when I was with Mike."

Holly touched her lips with her forefinger, shushing him. "I am my sister," she whispered. "Remember?"

"Sorry."

The door opened. A stocky man in his mid-forties stepped inside. He wore a pair of tan slacks, a blue-plaid dress shirt, and a cap with a bill that he seemed determined to keep on his head.

Suzann had already met him. Therefore, Holly pretended to know him too.

"I'm so glad you stopped by," Holly said. "Have you met Dr. McDowell?"

"We've met," both men said at once.

Bairn glared at Shawn. "Does he know why I'm here?"

"I told him you've been searching for my birth parents." Holly motioned toward a chair. "Please, sit down, Mr. Bairn." Suzann poured him a cup of coffee. "So, what have you come up with so far?"

He took the coffee, shaking his head. "Not much I'm afraid. I'm still searching for your birth mother, Ruth Ann Miller, but I'll need more money to follow up on another lead."

"What kind of money are we talking about?" she asked.

"I need to fly to Australia and stay there—" he shrugged "—a week, two. Maybe as long as a month."

"Why Australia?"

"The widow of the lawyer who drew up your adoption papers lives there now."

"I hadn't realized you even located Mr. Verde," she said, "much less that he had died."

"Well, he died, all right, and all his memories with him. But I'm hoping Mrs. Verde might know something."

"Wouldn't it be wise to phone her first?" Shawn put in. "Find out if she has any information before traveling all that way?"

"I'd do that," Mr. Bairn said, "if I thought Mrs. Verde would talk. However, it's been my experience that people clam up in cases like this. She might think I'm an insurance investigator or something. You never know."

"How much money will you need?" Holly asked.

Bairn shrugged. "Fifteen thousand ought to do it. Twenty if I have to stay longer than a month."

"I think ten thousand should be adequate," Holly said.

"That would hardly pay for my round-trip airfare."

"Go economy," Holly said. "That's what I do."

Bairn laughed and put down his cup. "I saw you in several romantic comedies, Miss Condry. But until now, I never realized you could be so funny, off camera."

"I don't believe Miss Condry is trying to be funny," Shawn said soberly. "I think she's quite serious."

Mr. Bairn stood. "I'll send you a detailed account

of my expenses when I return from Australia, Miss Condry, like I always do.''

"We'll talk about that after you phone Mrs. Verde and see if she'll agree to talk to you.''

"I'll do whatever I can.''

"And another thing,'' Holly said. "A reporter followed me to church tonight and took pictures. I think he knew I would be there. Do you happen to know anything about that?''

"Why would I? I'm not being paid to find out something like that.''

"You're being paid as my private investigator. Doesn't that mean you're supposed to find out anything I want to know?''

Bairn nodded reluctantly.

"Right now, I want to know how that reporter knew I'd be at that church.''

"I'll see what I can find out.''

After Bairn left, Shawn continued to study Holly, shaking his head from side to side the whole time.

"Okay, Dr. McDowell. What did I do wrong this time?''

"Movie stars are followed constantly,'' Shawn said. "Suzann Condry would know that.''

"I never thought—''

"Obviously. Besides, Bairn was hired to find your birth parents. If you want a shadow, you might have to consider hiring someone else.''

"You mean two private investigators?''

"Exactly.''

She considered his words carefully before continuing. "You could be right. Any suggestions?''

"Maybe. Let me do some checking first."

"I'm glad you were here when Mr. Bairn came by," Holly said. "I don't trust that man."

"Neither do I."

Chapter Eight

Suzann sat in a straight-backed chair in the church's fellowship hall, waiting for the Wednesday night service to begin. She had never intended to spend Thanksgiving at Josh's ranch. But each time he questioned her about it, she was distracted. Now with only a little over a week to decide, she realized she never had given Josh an unequivocal "no" to his kind invitation.

She also realized something else. She failed to mention Kate's invitation, and Josh Gallagher was headed straight for her. If she hoped to quell the debate just ahead, she would need to come up with a plan.

"So," he said, "you're going, aren't you?"

She produced a startled stare. "Going where?"

"To the ranch, of course, to have Thanksgiving at my parents' house and watch the Turkey game."

"Who's side is the turkey on?" she asked.

"Texas A&M's side, who else?"

"Sorry. I'll be rooting for the stuffing."

He laughed. "Stuffing?"

How could she have forgotten something as important as the fact that in the South the word was *dressing*, not stuffing?

"Of course I meant to say 'dressing,'" she said.

"That's better. For a minute, there, I thought I had a Yankee on my hands."

"Perish the thought."

Another warm chuckle, together with his usual boyish charm, sent her pulse racing. "Did I mention that Kate and her family will be having Thanksgiving dinner at our ranch too?" he asked.

"No, you didn't, but Kate did."

"Kate?"

"I'll be driving up on that Thursday morning with her."

A pained look of disappointment and frustration briefly clouded his features. "Oh? She didn't tell me."

"Actually," Suzann explained, "I thought I would stay over and spend Thursday night with Kate and her folks. Drive back Friday—or maybe wait until Saturday. But nothing's definite yet." She tossed back her hair. "So what are your plans?"

"Frankly, I don't have any. At least not now."

Suzann smiled, hoping to cheer him up. "Is there anything you would like me to bring?"

"Oh, no. Mom will have everything under control."

"Then I'll just pack my appetite."

"Yes." He turned to go. "'Cause Mom's a great cook."

Kate had said that Pastor Jones was out of town. Josh would be preaching that night. Suzann had hoped to ask him about it. She wouldn't get to now. She watched until he turned the corner, disappearing down the main hall.

The church was packed with young women and teenage girls that Suzann had never seen in church previously.

"Where did all these women come from?" Suzann whispered to Kate in the choir seat beside her. "It smells like the perfume department at Beaumonts," she added, fanning the air with her sheet music.

"Word must have gotten around that Josh is preaching tonight, what else?"

"I've never heard him," Suzann said, "but I had no idea he was that good."

"He's a good preacher, all right, but that's not what brought the females here, and you know it. Surely you've noticed how handsome he is."

Suzann rolled her eyes upward, toward the steepled roof. "Hush, Kate. Someone will hear you. Besides, the service is about to begin."

Thirty spine-tingling minutes later, Josh stepped up to the podium. A hush fell over the entire congregation. Suzann thought it was because all those strange women from other churches were holding their breaths.

"Brothers and sisters," Josh said, "tonight I would like to discuss the relationship between a Christian man and a Christian woman."

Suzann took in a big breath of her own and had no immediate plans to release it. She was glad Josh had his back to the choir and couldn't see her.

"Turn with me," he continued, "to the book of Genesis, chapter twenty-nine, verses ten and eleven. 'And it came to pass, when Jacob saw Rachel the daughter of Laban his mother's brother, that Jacob went near, and rolled the stone from the well's mouth, and watered the flock of Laban his mother's brother.'" Josh turned and faced the choir. Looking straight at Suzann, he smiled tenderly. "'And Jacob kissed Rachel.'" Josh turned back to the congregation then and started reading from the Bible again. "'And lifted up his voice, and wept.'"

Kate elbowed Suzann. "Did you catch that?"

"Catch what?"

Kate grinned. "You know as well as I do."

Suzann touched her lips with her forefinger.

"What do you think Jacob thought when he saw his future wife for the first time?" Josh asked. "I mean, what did each of you men out there think the first time you saw yours? I don't have a wife yet but..."

At that instant, Suzann figured that half the women she saw that night were in danger of fainting from sheer emotion alone.

"If I had a wife," he continued, "I think I would recognize her as the love of my life the instant I first saw her—just like Jacob did. Perhaps I would even kiss her."

Suzann's heart fell. The first time Josh Gallagher saw Holly Harmon, it was the real Holly—not her twin, Suzann Condry. In Suzann's mind, Josh couldn't have said he loved Holly more if he'd inserted her name in his sermon.

"Or," he added, "maybe I wouldn't really notice her at first—until suddenly—*bam*. The old heart starts pumping, and I suddenly realize that she is the one God intended for me to marry." He paused.

Suzann assumed he was either praying or reading from the Bible.

"In either case," Josh said, "I would know my future wife, and it would be right. You see, I believe that God designed one woman for every man—just like He designed Eve for Adam. And if a young man will pray, sooner or later the Lord will put just the right woman in his path."

Suzann hardly heard the rest of the sermon. As soon as the service ended, she changed out of her choir robe and hurried to her car.

Josh loved her sister. If she was lucky, Suzann could be halfway home before Josh started looking for her. What became perfectly clear to her was that she needed to get away, and her apartment wasn't nearly far enough.

Tomorrow was Thursday, her day off. What if she packed a few things and drove into San Antonio that very night? She could spend the night in a motel, shop the next day, and maybe take in a movie on Thursday night before driving back to Oak Valley. The more she thought about it, the more appealing the idea seemed.

Thirty minutes later she pulled away from the curb

and turned Holly's compact car in the direction of San Antonio.

Josh was too late to intercept Suzann at the church parking lot. However, he had every intention of following her home in order to explain about the sermon. Josh was beginning to think that the church librarian might be his "Rachel." He wanted to tell her exactly how he felt before he lost his nerve.

Suzann slept late the next morning. When she finally dressed, she went out and bought a black wig. Shopping in San Antonio was a joy. Yet when she passed by a Christian bookshop, she found herself going in and buying several Christian books and tapes. She also purchased a book on identical twins.

This would never do. Even with a black wig, she was still Holly Harmon. She had to do something drastic before it was too late.

She couldn't be Suzann Condry, openly, without wrecking her sister's life. Yet she wanted to step back into her old shoes, if only for an instant.

Wanted? Temporarily, she *craved* Tinsel Town.

Life as Holly Harmon was too inhibiting. Oh, she remembered her lines well enough. She just didn't like the script. She required a furlough from her vacation, a brief reprieve, or she would go nuts.

Suzann took the Bandera exit and sped out of the city limits of San Antonio, losing herself among the hills. A little after six, her stomach informed her it was time to head back to the city and she found her way to a small, comfortable-looking restaurant.

She was anticipating the steak she'd ordered when

she happened to notice a man watching her from a table nearby. Had he recognized her—even in the wig? She'd played a woman with raven hair in the movies.

Maybe she only imagined his interest in her.

Her head was spinning like a top. She realized that she hadn't eaten for hours. Suzann shook her head, hoping to clear her mind.

The man emerged from his chair and started toward her. "I've been watching you since you came in," he said, "and I find you extremely attractive. Have we met somewhere?"

"I doubt it." She tried not to laugh at the oldest line in the book. "I've rarely been to San Antonio, and I'll be leaving as soon as I've had my dinner," she added pointedly.

"Why don't I join you? Maybe I can persuade you to stick around a little longer. You might like it here."

"If you sit down at my table, I'll scream."

"Okay. No reason to panic," he assured her.

He gave a sly smile as he turned and walked off, and Suzann felt a shiver of fear. The waiter arrived with her steak. It smelled scrumptious, and as soon as she started eating, she forgot about the man with the beady brown eyes and green tweed suit. When she finished her dinner and walked through the café toward the exit, she noticed the man was nowhere in sight. He must have left while she was eating.

Outside, the street was well lit. Still, she almost wished she was on her way back to Oak Valley instead of walking through a strange town at night, looking for her car.

As she proceeded farther down the sidewalk, she caught sight of a dark-haired man in a green suit, standing in a doorway across the street. Her heart pounded. It was him. Even across the darkened street, she knew for sure when he waved at her. Suzann turned back around and took a deep breath. There was a way out of this. She just hadn't found it yet. If she could only make it to her car, she'd have a chance.

She charged toward the parking lot, then glanced back. The man had crossed the street and was running too.

Her heart tightened to a hard ball. Her breathing came in big gasps. Suzann wanted to look back again. Yet she knew if she did, she would find that he was gaining on her.

She could hear his footfalls, moving closer and closer. She wouldn't make it to the parking lot without being caught. But a church was straight ahead.

The double doors were wide open. She'd just seen two women go in. Well, she would go in too.

She chose a pew near the back behind a huge stone pillar, where she wouldn't be easily seen. And there was always the chance that he would decide not to follow her in.

The women were praying at an altar to one side of the main sanctuary. Unless she dashed out of her hiding place and made herself known, they would be no help at all. Suzann shivered. The rest of the church was empty.

As she sat there, trembling, she began to hope. Was he gone for good? Had he lost interest in her? It was possible.

She was beginning to feel secure. Then someone tapped her on the shoulder from behind.

She jerked forward.

"Well," she heard him say, "so we meet again."

Her body stiffened. It was him.

"I never expected to find you here," he added. "So how was your steak, sweet thing? Mine was great."

With a sudden burst of courage, Suzann whirled around in her pew, planning to sock her attacker in the face.

"I wouldn't try that if I were you," he said.

She opened her mouth to scream. Her clenched fist froze in midpunch. He had a knife.

"That's better."

He reached out and took hold of her wrist with one hand.

Suzann trembled. "Please, let me go," she said in a shaky voice. "I promise not to turn you in."

"Not a chance."

He rubbed the side of the knife against her slender throat. The blade felt slick and cold on her skin.

A silent shudder ran the length of her body. Don't hurt me, she pleaded silently. Suzann opened her mouth to scream.

He put his hand over her mouth. Then he leaned over and whispered. "Just so you'll know exactly what's going to happen to you," he said, "we're going to sit right here until those women leave the church. Don't move an inch or try to scream again. Or you'll be sorry."

Frozen with fear, Suzann realized that she wanted, *needed* to pray—except that she didn't know how.

She hadn't prayed since she was a small child. Nevertheless, she intended to try. Immediately.

Our Father who art in Heaven, she prayed. *I can't remember the rest of this prayer, and I don't know any other prayers. But if You'll help me escape from that man, I promise to learn how to pray. Amen.*

A big man in a policeman's uniform came around from behind the stone pillar and pulled out a gun. Had God heard her prayer?

"Take your hands off the woman," the policeman ordered, "and put them in the air. You're under arrest."

"He's got a knife!" Suzann shouted.

"Hand it over—" the policeman cocked his gun with a click "—or you're history."

The man paused for what seemed like forever. Then he released her and handed the knife to the policeman.

Suzann held her breath until the policeman handcuffed the criminal and read him his rights.

"Would you mind coming down to the station house, ma'am, and signing a complaint form?"

"Do I have to?" Suzann asked.

"It sure would help." The policeman's voice was kind, gentle. "I heard most of what he said to you, but not all of it. You could help fill in the blank spaces."

"All I really want—" Her voice highlighted the tears she was trying so hard to conceal. "All I—" She sniffed, wiping her eyes. "I just want to get in my car and drive on home."

"I can understand that, ma'am. But if you signed

that complaint form first, it would put this creep behind bars where he belongs.''

Suzann shrugged helplessly. "I guess I'll do it,
then. Will it take long?"

"Not very. And I really appreciate your taking the
time. I've been trying to catch this guy for months.
But I never figured I'd catch him here. Frankly, I
came in to pray before going off duty, not to look for
this guy."

"I prayed too." Suzann rubbed the tears from the
edges of her eyes with the back of her hand. "For the
first time in ages."

"Praying helps, doesn't it?" the policeman said.

"You bet it helps."

Though she tried hard to hide it, the emotional im-
pact of what had happened at the church was a fear
and foreboding beyond anything she'd ever known.
She shook so hard on the drive to the police station
in the squad car that Officer Edwards suggested that
she phone someone to come and drive her home. But
under the circumstances, who could she possibly call?

"I'll be all right," she'd said, "as soon as I get
home." But Suzann wasn't all right. She didn't know
if she ever would be again.

Later, as she drove down the highway toward Oak
Valley, she began to wonder if it was prayer that had
saved her—or pure luck. By the time she arrived at
her apartment, she was convinced that she'd merely
been extremely fortunate.

After all, it wasn't God who actually saved her. Just
that nice Officer Edwards who happened to be nearby.

* * *.

Suzann was so nervous and upset the next morning, because of what had happened in San Antonio, that she called in sick. She also missed all Sunday services as well. On the Monday before Thanksgiving, she forced herself to return to work.

She'd meant to visit the shops on the other side of the hill at noon that day. Now she wasn't sure when she would find the courage to go sightseeing again.

Once she had claimed to be almost fearless, but that was merely a mask to hide behind. She'd been a fraidy-cat since, since— When had it started? When had this "I hate to be alone in the dark and in empty buildings" thing first begun?

The name Dexter Quin, child actor, flashed on her memory screen. Unlike the Dexter that was a preacher in Dallas, Dexter Quin had always meant trouble. Suzann first knew the child when they were both ten years old and making a movie together. She'd wanted to give him the benefit of the doubt—until he locked her in a dark storage room, and she wasn't found for two hours.

Perhaps years of hard work and very little time off was also partly to blame for her faintheartedness. No wonder Holly had suggested six months in Oak Valley. Her twin must have sensed Suzann's stressed-out state.

She intended to get over these crippling fears of hers. But she wanted to take it slowly—one day at a time. Until she felt more like her old self again, she would do only those chores that she absolutely had to do. She also planned to avoid going out alone at night whenever possible.

Merely driving the three blocks to the Dizzy Dairy for lunch on Monday caused a shudder deep within her. On her way back to the church library, she stopped off at the post office to check her mail.

A package from her agent, Mike McDowell, waited in her private mailbox. Ripping off the brown envelope, she found a screenplay with a message from Mike written on the title page.

I know I promised not to send you any more scripts, but this movie was made for you. It's a Roland Grant Production. Todd Kemper will produce. Vance Wilds will direct, and both Todd and Vance sounded interested in putting you in the female lead.

Steve Norton has the male lead in the bag, Suzann, and I know you and Steve have always worked well together. So what more could you want? Not only that, but they won't even start filming for another six months.

You could easily stay in Oak Valley the full time and still do the picture. I really think this is that big chance you've waited for all your life, Sue. Don't throw it away on a whim.

Mike

Mike McDowell might not be the greatest person in the world, she thought. But he's still the best agent around. It couldn't have been easy to swing a deal like this one. Yet he'd managed to do it.

Excitement coursed through her as Suzann glanced down at the title page again, granting her a temporary reprieve from her distressed state. *A Time to Love*. Interesting title, and starring Steve Norton.

Steve was a sweetheart and a dream to work with. Mike was right. What more could she want?

She slipped the manuscript back in what was left of the envelope before anyone saw it. She could hardly wait to read the script. If she went right back to the library, she could start reading immediately.

At the library half an hour later, it became clear that the plot and the theme were flawless. The role of Elizabeth Winters was Academy Award material and far above every character Suzann had ever played. She wanted, *needed* this part.

Yet the thought of playing love scenes with Steve Norton alarmed her. The question was, why? She'd played scenes like that in the past, plenty of times.

What was happening to her? Was Suzann Condry still in there somewhere? She was beginning to wonder. She put the manuscript in her big purse.

Later, as Suzann was putting some books back on the shelf, she recalled again what happened in San Antonio. She'd calmed down just enough to begin dusting one of the bookcases, when Josh came in.

Merely seeing him again invoked a mood of excitement. She pushed it back determinedly, hoping he would assume that she couldn't care less.

"Josh, what are you doing here?" she asked. "I thought the pastors were in a meeting all afternoon."

"The meeting hasn't started yet." He moved to her side, resting his left elbow on the bookcase she'd been dusting. "Got a minute?"

Plainly, she hadn't discouraged him.

"It's important," he added.

"All right." Suzann looked away, so those blue eyes of his wouldn't sidetrack her thinking. Then she sat down in the chair behind her desk. "Won't you sit down?"

He settled into the empty chair across from hers.

"What's so important?" she asked.

"I want to know why you went to San Antonio without telling anybody. That's so unlike you."

"I haven't *felt* much like me lately. Maybe I'm coming down with something again."

"Don't kid around." His jaw firmed up defensively. "I was worried about you, and so was Kate."

"I'm touched, really. But I have a perfect right to drive into San Antonio anytime I want to—and you know it."

"Kate said that a man followed you." He lifted his chin resolutely. "You could have been…" His deep voice slowly diminished and was replaced by a long silence.

She sensed that he'd made some kind of decision. She needed to keep her guard up.

"Who can say what might have happened to an attractive, young woman alone in a big city?" he added finally.

"Kate should never have told you about that."

"She was worried."

"You said that."

"So was I."

"You said that too." Suzann delivered a sigh born of frustration. "Look, nothing happened, okay? I'm fine."

"Are you sure?" His gaze interrogated her with an intensity that was almost physical. "You looked upset when I first came in. Maybe you should talk to Pastor Jones about this."

She merely shook her head.

"Oh, I forgot. You're the female who handles her own problems, aren't you? Miss Independent," he said sarcastically. "Frankly, I think you need to learn to lean a little—on Jesus and on the people who care about you."

She gazed down at the papers on her desk. He was getting too close, pushing her too hard. She almost wished she'd stayed in San Antonio. If not for the man in the green suit, she might have.

"I have a lot of work to do, Josh, and you have a meeting to attend. Why don't we put this discussion on hold until we've both had time to cool down?"

"Okay." His facial expression still held a trace of annoyance, but he'd managed to tone it down slightly. "But we *will* discuss this again."

"All right. But I really can't see the point."

"I care what happens to you, Holly Harmon." A tender gleam intertwined with his stern-faced expression. "That's the *point* in all this."

I really think you do care, she thought. Too bad my name is Suzann Condry.

"I care what happens to you too, Josh. Christians are designed to care. That's what Christianity is all about, isn't it?"

"Yes," he said reflectively, "that's part of what it's all about. It's the other part that's still unsettled."

He turned, then, and left the library, slamming the glass door behind him.

She wanted to open her heart to Josh. She'd thought about it. Considered. *What would be the harm?* But if she opened her heart to him, even a crack, she doubted that she would ever be able to shut it again.

Chapter Nine

Holly smiled at her reflection in the full-length mirror in the master bedroom. Turning to the side, she concluded that her diet must have worked. The silver dress fit perfectly now.

Mike had other plans for the evening, he'd said. Dr. Shawn McDowell waited downstairs to take her to her first opening, and that suited Holly just fine.

When she thought about it, she surmised that this was her first real opportunity to present herself as Suzann Condry. What happened at the church with the cameraman didn't count. The question was, could she pull it off?

Holly grabbed Suzann's diamond-crested handbag and left the room. Her sister had said that the expressions on her fans' faces often told exactly how she stood with them. As soon as she arrived at the hotel where the opening was being held and stepped out of the limo, she would know whether or not she shone as a believable Suzann Condry.

Shawn stood at the bottom of the stairs, looking more handsome than Holly thought possible. A warm thrill rushed through her on seeing him in his black tux, scarlet-velvet vest, and black tie.

His face lit up when he saw her. His tender grin knocked at the door of her heart. Yet it was his blue-green eyes, gleaming with appreciation as he took in her appearance from head to toe, that sent her senses into orbit.

She sucked in her breath. If the rise and fall of her breathing got any louder, he would hear it.

Shawn still hadn't said that he cared for her. However, if she was reading his expression correctly, he did. So what was stopping him from telling her? Did he think she would be offended? Or was there another reason?

"You look great," he said. "But are you ready for this?"

Holly lifted her head. "I'm ready." She endeavored to hide her excitement on seeing him again by manufacturing a soft smile. "And you look great, too."

"Frankly, I feel out of place in this monkey suit."

She laughed. "Nonsense." She offered him her white-gloved arm. "Shall we go?"

"Let's."

The mere thought of all those people gawking at her, caused her heart to compress and knot long before they reached the hotel. In the glare of bright lights and flashing cameras, she estimated that all her insides weighed a ton. By the time she and Shawn reached the huge auditorium, she was sure of it.

She'd smiled for the cameras. She really had. She had also tried to repress all winsome gazes. But judging from the surprised looks some members of the press gave her, that wide-eyed stare of hers had reappeared.

"You're doing great," Shawn whispered perceptively.

"I'm not sure I can go through with this, Shawn."

"Remember what Suzann said. Just call everybody 'dar-ling.'"

She fluttered her eyelashes. "Thank you, dar-ling, for reminding me."

"Don't mention it." He winked.

She realized that Shawn was teasing her in the hope of relaxing her, and so far, it was working.

Mike walked by, escorting a beautiful blonde with a high-pitched laugh. Holly blinked. So this was the "other plans" he had for the evening....

Cameras rolled. Holly tried to ignore them as she and Shawn headed for the reserved section near the stage. She'd barely settled into her seat when Greer Fraser came up and knelt in the aisle beside her.

Surprised, she nearly swallowed her tongue. Besides Suzann, Greer was the first real-for-sure movie star she'd ever seen, close up. And he just happened to be her favorite actor.

"Hi, gorgeous," Greer said. "I noticed you when you came in, and you look fantastic." He sent Shawn a brief nod. "Dr. McDowell, good to see you again." Greer turned back to Holly. "It's been too long, Sue. May I call you?"

Greer looked better in person than he did on the

movie screen. For an instant, Holly wanted to say "yes" in spite of all Suzann's warnings to the contrary.

"Frankly," Holly said coolly, "I doubt that I'll be home."

"I'll risk it." Greer reached for her hand and squeezed it. "See ya." And then he was gone.

Shawn cleared his throat. Then he ran his forefinger under his collar. "I think you handled that very well, considering. Will you be taking his calls?"

Holly shook her head. "Bates will."

He leaned over to whisper in her ear, and a thrill tingled through her. "Everybody within earshot is watching us," he whispered. "And I saw the video cameras zoom in on that little scene between you and Greer."

Looking up at Shawn, she faked her best movie-star smile. "I'm so glad you like my dress," she said loudly enough for everyone nearby to hear. "I'll be sure to tell my designer."

"You always seem to know just the right thing to say, Miss Condry. How do you manage?"

Her smile deepened. "Oh, years of practice, I guess."

The house lights dimmed. The emcee came on stage.

"You're amazing." Shawn took her hand in his and held it. "Keep it up."

"I plan to, Doctor," she said.

Suzann would have thoroughly enjoyed driving through the Texas hills on that Thanksgiving morning were it not for what had happened in San Antonio. She still couldn't get that night out of her mind. Nevertheless, she'd always loved the autumn season and meant to enjoy herself as Kate's guest for the weekend.

"Are you all right?" Kate asked. "You looked troubled there for a minute. I was wondering if you were still thinking about what happened at that church in San Antonio."

Suzann turned toward her friend and nodded slowly. "I guess maybe I am thinking about it more than I should."

"Why don't you talk to Pastor Jones? He's good at talking to people with problems."

Suzann paused solicitously. "Maybe I will," she said, then changed the subject. "I trust that your father is continuing to recover from his recent heart attack."

"Yes, he is," Kate said, "and thanks for asking."

Though Kate had invited the real Holly to visit her home many times, Holly never had. As a result, Suzann wouldn't have to pretend she knew every person or landmark she saw during her Thanksgiving holiday. Still, it didn't seem fair, visiting the two ranches before Holly had the opportunity to visit them.

Many of the fall leaves had already fled the trees for the ground below. Still, the trees and bushes glowed with even more fall colors than Suzann had seen on the day she arrived in Oak Valley. Kate motioned toward a rustic gate with an iron brand over the top.

"That's where Josh lives," she said.

"That's the Chula Vista?"

Kate nodded. "Or rather, that's where you turn off to go to the headquarters of his Chula Vista Ranch."

"His?"

"Well, his parents own it now. But someday the ranch will be his."

"Chula Vista," Suzann repeated. "That means pretty view, doesn't it?"

"Yes," Kate said, "and if you like trees, clear running water, and autumn hills as much as I think you do, you're going to love the ranch."

"I never doubted it for a minute." Suzann smiled. "How far are we from your ranch?"

"Not far. In fact, the Lazy-D connects to the Gallagher place. Just a barbwire fence between us."

"I guess your family and the Gallagher family must have become close during the years."

"My, yes, in fact—"

Suzann sensed that Kate wanted to say more. She questioned why she didn't.

"As you know," Kate said slowly, "we always either spent Thanksgiving with the Gallaghers or they came to our ranch and spent it with us. We've been doing that forever, I think."

"It must be nice to have close friends like that."

"I guess you and your parents must have a lot of friends too where you live," Kate said.

"Oh, oh yes, we do."

"I suppose you visited your family during your recent vacation."

Suzann nodded, hating the lie. Kate had been asking a lot of hard-to-answer questions lately.

"And that reminds me," Suzann said. "How's your job at the law office? You didn't seem too happy there the last time we discussed it."

"I'm thinking of quitting."

"Quitting your job?"

"Why not?"

"I don't know. I'm just surprised, I guess. What will you do?"

"I'm not sure. Maybe I'll pull up stakes, go back to Saint Mary's in San Antonio, and finish college."

"Your degree's in nutrition, isn't it?"

"It *was*."

"And if you go back?"

Kate looked down the road ahead. "I'll major in law."

"You want to become a lawyer?"

"I do now."

"Oh, Kate, that's wonderful. What changed your mind?"

"A lot of things. Maybe I'll tell you about them someday." Kate motioned toward another rustic gate. "That's the Lazy-D, just ahead." She slowed in order to make the turn.

"I can hardly wait to see it."

As they drove down the tree-lined, country road to ranch headquarters, Suzann contemplated Kate's recent behavior. First, she'd been full of questions. Now she seemed detached, almost unapproachable. Her friend was acting strangely, and Suzann wondered why.

The log house sat on a hill and was at least a mile

from the main highway. Suzann loved the Lazy-D instantly.

She also liked Kate's parents—William and Alice Devlon—Kate's German shepherd, Grumpy, and her girlish bedroom with the white lace curtains and canopy bed.

After Suzann had raved about everything, Kate finally asked, "Is there anything you *don't* like?"

"I don't think so. Check again later, and I'll let you know for sure."

"Then why don't I leave you here in my bedroom to decide," Kate said, "while I go down and see if Mother needs anything? We'll be packing the van for the drive to Chula Vista in about twenty minutes. Until then, there are always last-minute chores to do."

"Please, let me go down and help."

"You're my guest. Besides, Mom seems to have everything under control. But I noticed she was making a salad tray. And if I know my mother, she'll want me to open a jar of pickles or something."

"Is that your job around here?"

Kate's smile seemed forced, somehow, as if she was still hiding something. "I open jars that stick, fix leaky sinks, and I do windows when I have to."

"Are you sure you wouldn't like a helper, standing in the background—giving you unsolicited advice?"

"Positive."

"In that case, I guess I'll stay here and enjoy this gorgeous room of yours."

"That's an excellent idea. Glad I thought of it."

When Kate had left the room, Suzann went over to the glassed-in, wooden showcase to inspect Kate's numerous barrel riding trophies and high school mementos. Out of the corner of her eye she noticed a photograph on Kate's dressing table of a young man, probably of high school age, wearing a football uniform.

Even at a distance, the young man looked extremely handsome. She couldn't resist going over and reading the signature under the picture.

To Kate, it read, *a sensible female, and the only cowgirl I'd ever consider marrying. Love, Josh.*

So Kate and Josh had been high school sweethearts—or at the least, very close. Why wasn't she told? This revelation hurt.

Was this the secret Kate hadn't wanted Suzann or Holly to know? Obviously, Josh and Kate were no longer dating. But did Kate still care for Josh? Was that the reason she kept silent?

Suzann had expected more from a Christian. Kate should have been honest from the very beginning instead of pretending that she and Josh were never more than childhood playmates.

Suzann hadn't realized that she was still staring at Josh's photograph. She forced her gaze downward, toward the blue carpet. Her sister's words floated back to her.

Mrs. Beesley said that Josh has a girlfriend who lives on a ranch near his ranch, and his parents hope he will marry her someday.

Kate was the girlfriend Holly had been talking about. Only at the time, Holly didn't know it.

In Tinsel Town, friends were few and far between. But Suzann thought she'd found a true friend in Kate

Devlon. She should have known their friendship was too good to be true.

"I'm sorry you saw that picture," Kate said from the doorway.

Suzann froze, determined to choose her words carefully. Not only had Kate returned to the bedroom, but she'd caught her admiring Josh's photograph.

"I packed that picture away a long time ago," Kate added. "I had no idea Mom would unpack it and set it on my dressing table while I was away."

Suzann recovered enough to give an indifferent shrug. "So?"

"I was afraid you might be upset."

"Why should I be?" Suzann cocked her head to one side, forcing a smile. "Josh Gallagher means nothing to me. Besides, that was then and this is now."

Kate studied her searchingly—as if she knew more was going on than Suzann was willing to admit. "I wish I'd noticed the picture when we first came in," Kate said, "but I didn't. And you'll never know how sorry I am. But let's not let this little incident spoil Thanksgiving for everybody."

"Why should it?"

"It shouldn't—unless you care more for Josh Gallagher than you say you do."

"What are you driving at?"

"I was afraid you might feel more for Josh than you've let on so far."

"Nonsense." Suzann blinked. Okay, it's true, she thought.

She *was* interested in Josh Gallagher, but their relationship was going nowhere. Beyond that, it was a matter of trust.

Suzann had believed in Kate and their friendship, and Kate had disappointed her. Kate hadn't lived up to her idea of what a Christian was supposed to be. And why hadn't Josh mentioned that he and Kate dated when they were in high school?

Suzann's own dishonesty hit her then like a hard punch to the belly. With her own shortcomings and outright lies, she was hardly in a position to look down on someone else.

Still, Josh and Kate's lack of openness cut her emotionally. She'd been betrayed before, plenty of times, but never by people who supposedly strove to be loving and honest.

"Can you ever forgive me?" Kate asked finally.

"Sure, why wouldn't I?"

"I don't know." Kate gave a helpless shrug. "You just don't look very forgiving right now."

Suzann tried to laugh it off. "Thanks a lot."

"Sorry," Kate said. "I never meant that as an insult."

"No problem."

Suzann felt suddenly uncomfortable. The thought of spending two days with Kate and her family did not sound appealing. She yearned for an excuse to get away. Finding one would not be easy.

Slowly, the animated expression Suzann had manufactured earlier fell away. She touched her stomach, feigning a facial expression she hoped made her look extremely unwell.

"Are you all right?" Kate asked.

"I guess so." Suzann shook her head. "To be perfectly honest, no."

"You're ill?"

Suzann nodded. "Frankly, I'm really not feeling well at all."

"I'm so sorry to hear that." Kate sent her a sympathetic glance. "I guess we could stay here instead of going to the Gallagher ranch for dinner."

"No, I wouldn't want you to miss your Thanksgiving meal on my account."

"Then what do you suggest we do?" Kate asked.

"I could be feeling better in an hour or two."

"I certainly hope so."

"If not, maybe Josh will be kind enough to drive me back to Oak Valley tonight." Suzann produced a weak smile. "But let's not talk about that possibility now, okay?"

"Whatever you say."

Here I go again, Suzann thought, adding still more sins to the ones I already have stacked up.

According to Pastor Jones, Jesus died for her sins so she could be forgiven for them. Would Suzann ever be able to tell little white lies again without feeling guilty?

Chapter Ten

Suzann and Kate sat in the back seat on the drive to Josh's home. She'd searched in vain for the bright small talk any Hollywood celebrity knew by heart, but found nothing. Kate hadn't had much to say either.

The van rolled under the arch above the gate, and they entered the Chula Vista Ranch. A big, two-story stone house on a hill loomed in the distance.

Kate's mother turned to them. "Y'all are mighty quiet back there."

Suzann smiled nervously without looking at Kate.

"Well, Miss Harmon," Mrs. Devlon continued, "what do you think of the Chula Vista so far?"

"I think it's beautiful here."

"Wait 'til you see the house. And the river out back is so clear you can see all the way to the bottom."

"I'm sure I'm going to love it, ma'am."

"Kate tells us that you like antiques. And you'll see plenty at the Chula Vista. That's for sure."

"I'm looking forward to that, too," Suzann said.

Mrs. Devlon turned back around and clicked on the radio. A western tune blared, absorbing the silence that had hovered over them earlier.

"All right," Kate said finally. "I'll come clean."

Suzann blinked. "I beg your pardon."

"I'm still in love with Josh Gallagher, okay?"

Stunned, Suzann paused, anticipating what Kate might say next.

"Loving Josh is not something I'm proud of," Kate said, "because he's in love with you. I'm merely stating a fact. I took the job in the law office in Oak Valley in hopes of rekindling the flame, but it didn't work out. That's why I've decided to go back to college next term. So, now you know."

Suzann didn't know how to reply, nor did she want to say anything. But she did feel sorry for Kate. Reaching out, she patted Kate's shoulder just as Holly would have done if she'd been there.

Kate smiled at Suzann's gesture of comfort. "Thanks."

The only reply Suzann could muster was a half-hearted nod.

For Suzann, the process of forgiveness was starting at square one. She doubted it could progress to square two until she'd had time to consider all the implications.

Mr. Devlon slowed for the stop ahead, then parked in a space in front of the house to the left of the circle drive.

As she got out of the van, Suzann spied a trickle of water, rippling softly into a natural, rock-bottom pond to the right of the house. Trees and shrubs in fall colors dotted the front yard. A tree limb eerily scraped the wooden porch in front of the house.

A middle-aged woman in jeans and a bright red Western shirt came out to meet them. A tall gray-haired cowboy followed her. Plainly, this handsome couple were Josh's parents.

The house was all Kate's mother had said, and more. Suzann thought it looked like a picture straight from a house-and-garden magazine, complete with rustic, oak furniture and expensive antiques.

Spicy scents flowed from the country kitchen. Hanging Indian saddle blankets framed a huge stone fireplace. The polished skull of a Texas longhorn hung above a wooden mantle. A log stairway curved upward to an open loft to the right of the fireplace.

But where was Josh?

He appeared in the doorway leading to a hall. "Sorry I'm late," he said, "but I had some cowboying to do this morning. And I was all dirty. I think everybody will be glad I cleaned up first."

Kate held her nose teasingly. "I know *I'm* glad."

"Me too," Suzann said, then wished she'd kept silent.

Josh's mother offered Suzann a comfy chair to the right of the fireplace. Then his mother went into the kitchen. Kate settled into a chair across the room from Suzann's.

Suzann noticed a photograph on a lamp table nearby of Josh and Kate together. They were wearing formal attire and looked to be about seventeen or eighteen years old. Josh frowned when he saw her studying the picture.

She looked away, focusing on the fireplace. Josh moved to the right of the fireplace, propping his arm across the oak mantle. A glimmer of worry flashed in his eyes.

She felt trapped. Yet it would be awkward to look away with him watching her. Clearly, he knew that.

"How do you like Chula Vista?" he asked.

"It's really beautiful, exactly as I expected."

He glanced toward the photograph on the lamp table—then to the door leading to the patio. Was he inviting her to step outside with him to talk? She pretended not to understand his message, gazing instead at the carved arms of the antique chair next to hers.

He must have thought she was urging him to sit in that chair. In an instant, he was seated beside her.

Suzann grimaced. "We can't talk here," she whispered.

"Okay, we'll talk later then."

Mrs. Gallagher came back into the living room. "Okay, y'all. The turkey's ready. It's time to go in and eat. And would everyone mind smiling a little more, please. After all, this is Thanksgiving."

The meal tasted delicious. Suzann loved the cornbread dressing, but she didn't feel like eating much of it.

After dessert, the crowd drifted into the den to watch the Turkey Game between the University of Texas and Texas A&M. Suzann pretended to watch. Her thoughts were elsewhere.

During the halftime performance, Kate suggested that the young people go outside for a breath of air. Both sets of parents looked pleased, as if they thought Kate wanted to be with Josh.

As soon as they were out of earshot, Kate turned to Suzann. "Look, I know you two have things you need to say to each other. So how 'bout if I disappear for a while and leave y'all alone?"

Without another word, Kate crossed her arms over her pale pink sweater and walked off toward the old barn. Josh and Suzann watched until she went inside.

"I'd like to explain about that picture you saw on the lamp table," he said.

"That's not necessary."

"Yes it is. And you're going to listen," he said, "whether you want to or not."

Suzann pressed her lips together stubbornly. She hated it when Josh did his whether-you-want-to-or-not thing. Some might call it manly. After all that had happened that day, she didn't appreciate it.

Hands on his hips, he glared at her. "I was never in love with Kate Devlon."

"How sad." She glanced away. "She's a nice person."

"I know she is." He took hold of her chin, forcing her to look at him again. "And I think the world of her. In fact, she's one of my oldest and dearest friends. But my feelings for her have never been the kind that a man feels for a woman. We've always just been really good friends."

"What about Kate? Was it just friendship on her side too?"

"I'm sure it was." He shrugged. "Actually, I never asked."

"Maybe you should have."

He paused introspectively. "You could be right."

He took her hand, leading her to a wooden bench in front of a spreading Spanish oak. Rusty-red leaves had fallen on the seat of the bench. He brushed them away.

He sat down then pulled her down beside him. Dry leaves crunched under his cowboy boots. His right arm slipped around her shoulders possessively. A tender warmth enveloped her in spite of all her efforts to prevent it.

"Kate and I have always known each other," he said, "and our parents have let it be known that they have always hoped we would marry someday."

I know that, she thought.

"I dated a girl my parents disapproved of for a while when I was a senior in high school. At the time, I thought I was in love with her. Pam lived in another little town not far from here, and it was difficult to see her. She had her school functions to attend, and I had mine. Finally, we just drifted apart."

He sounded almost gloomy when he talked about his relationship with Pam. Suddenly the dark clouds in his eyes disappeared. A quick grin emerged.

"Actually," he said with a laugh, "she dumped me."

"And Kate was right there to pump you up, I'll bet."

"Yeah, and she was wonderful," he said. "So kind and understanding. For a while I thought it was Kate

I'd loved all along, and my parents encouraged those feelings.''

"Look, there's no reason for you to tell me all this.''

"There's a reason all right.'' His gaze zoomed in on her lips.

A sparkling kind of joy charged through her. Under the circumstances, she thought it might be best if she got him talking again.

"You were saying?''

"Oh, yes,'' he said. "I was explaining about Pam.'' His gaze still lingered on her mouth. "When I finally got over Pam, I knew I'd never really loved Kate. She was just there. I never meant to hurt her. And I sure hope I didn't.''

"And then?''

"We both went off to college. Kate went to Saint Mary's in San Antonio, and I went to Texas A&M.''

"Kate said you made the rodeo team there.''

"It was no big deal, believe me.'' He watched her for a moment as if he'd asked her a question that she wasn't answering. "And later,'' he continued, "I transferred to Baylor and switched my major from animal science to religion. That's when I became a preacher.''

"How did your parents feel about the switch?''

"They were disappointed, at first. I was supposed to run the ranch someday.'' He looked off at a pasture filled with red cattle and Angora goats. At last, he turned back to Suzann. "But my parents have learned to accept my ministry. Now I think they're kind of proud—in a way.''

"They should be. You're a fine person."

He smiled. "I'm warning you, compliments will get you anything you want from me."

"How about a ride back to Oak Valley after the football game?"

A puzzled frown flashed across his face. "I thought you were spending the weekend with Kate?"

"Those plans have changed."

"May I ask why?"

"No," she said lightly, "you may not ask why." She grinned. "Just kidding."

Suzann wasn't sick when she told Kate she was, and she wasn't ill now. But if she hoped to leave for Oak Valley before nightfall, she would have to tell another falsehood.

"I have a headache," Suzann said, "and from experience I know it's probably going to get worse. I thought I'd be more comfortable at home, if you wouldn't mind driving me there."

"I'd be glad to."

A slow smile surfaced. "Thanks." She glanced down at her watch. "I guess we should go back inside. The second half of that football game should be starting any minute."

Suzann was relieved when she finally reached Holly's apartment. Acting was one thing—pretending, another. She couldn't fit into a family like Josh's in a million years.

She also felt uneasy, even after locking all the doors and windows. Her apartment seemed safe enough but... She'd been trying to work through her memories of the man in the green suit. But thoughts of what happened in San Antonio just wouldn't go away.

Suzann flopped down on the blue couch. Removing her shoes, she propped her bare feet on the coffee table and wiggled her toes.

She was a poor excuse for a Christian. That was for sure. She couldn't even *play* one convincingly.

Could Holly be right? Did Suzann need God in her life?

Salvation would require a drastic change in her lifestyle. The mere thought of it frightened her.

No, she wouldn't, couldn't do anything that radical. However, she could become a kinder, gentler person. That wasn't something she deemed impossible to manage.

As a regular church-goer now, Suzann had witnessed several miracles. Just last week the Lord healed Mrs. Page, a lifelong member of Oak Valley Bible Church. And she was cured of cancer by the power of God.

As the evening progressed, Suzann continued to think about becoming a Christian in the true sense. Strangely, she couldn't read her Sunday School lesson for thinking about it. She also thought about Josh, of course, and she replayed in her mind all that had happened that day.

The phone rang.

Who would be calling her on Thanksgiving night? She smiled. Holly, of course. Her caller had to be her twin sister.

She reached for the receiver on the third ring.

"Hello."

"Hello, may I speak to Miss Holly Harmon, please."

"This is she."

"Miss Harmon, this is Officer Edwards. We met in San Antonio. Remember?"

Her heart raced. How could she forget? "It's nice to hear from you again, Officer," she said. "Anything wrong?"

"Not really. And I hate to be calling you on a holiday like this. But I pulled the holiday night shift and it's pretty slow. I thought you might like an update on the case. You said you wanted to know what happened to the guy that followed you."

"Yes, I do want to know. Please, tell me."

"Well, he's been involved in a lot of other crimes against women. He goes to trial in a few months. After that, I think he's going to be put away for a long time."

"That's a relief."

Suzann wondered if she would have to be involved in some way. But how could she be? The name on the driver's license, Holly Harmon, that she used at the police station in San Antonio wasn't even her real name.

"I was wondering," Suzann said, "will I have to testify?"

"Not unless you want to," he said. "We have plenty of witnesses with more to tell about this guy than you do."

"Then if you don't mind, I think I'll just stay out

of it. I live in a little town here, and I'm the church librarian.''

"You said you were a librarian that night down at the station," the officer said. "But you know what?" He chuckled softly. "The cops here all think you look a lot like that movie star, Suzann Condry. Ever heard of her?"

"Yes," she said, "and thanks for the compliment."

"Don't mention it." He laughed again. "If you're ever in San Antonio and in the neighborhood, stop by the station and see us, ma'am. Some of the guys around here want your autograph."

Chapter Eleven

Holly had trembled openly as Shawn ushered her through the crush of reporters waiting in front of the convention center when they arrived. Even now, when she was reasonably safe, she shook internally. She wouldn't have made it without Shawn.

Since the fund-raiser was being held on the Saturday after Thanksgiving, Holly hadn't expected much press coverage. How wrong could she be?

The writers and photojournalists she saw when they first stepped out of the limo had reminded her of a bunch of cave dwellers seeking a prey. Grabbing. Pushing.

Apparently since the opening, word had gotten out that Suzann Condry was different somehow. The conventional press was reporting that presumably she'd found faith. Now everybody wanted to interview her, refusing to give up until they did.

The fund-raiser was being held in the banquet hall off the main reception area. Until then, Holly was expected to go into a small studio and make a short video to be used as a television commercial. Getting to that location seemed impossible.

Then Shawn, his arm around her shoulders, side-tracked the reporters and photojournalists, delivering her to her destination on time and all in one piece. Amazing.

The press were demanding an interview with her. Holly and Shawn managed to slip into the studio and lock the door behind them. At least behind locked doors, they were somewhat protected from the pack of wolves outside.

A small group of photographers and cameramen waited in Studio B. After a quick run-through, the cameras rolled, and Holly completed "take one" of the video. She hadn't expected takes two, three or four.

Shawn must have known how nervous she felt because he had nothing but praise for her performance. Still, she knew she'd been a poor excuse for Suzann Condry, no matter what Shawn said to the contrary.

At last one of the cameramen informed her that the fourth take was a print. She'd disliked the taping session. The strain of it left her feeling shaky and apprehensive. When everybody but Shawn left the studio, Holly went over and bolted the door.

Shawn was leaning against a desk near the door. When Holly walked by, he pulled her into his arms. His gentle, blue-green gaze caressed her tenderly. "Feeling better?"

"A little."

Holly clenched and unclenched her fist as a wave

of nerves swept over her. She loved being in Shawn's arms, but she felt so jittery that she couldn't keep still long enough to enjoy it.

"You're shaking," he said.

"I think I need to sit down." She moved out of his embrace, settling into a chair. "I know I'll feel a lot better when I get that speech behind me."

"You'll sound terrific." Shawn put his briefcase on the desk, removing a pen and a notepad. "Now—" he grinned "—I want you to tell me your birth mother's name again so I can write it down."

"Sorry, I'm not in the mood."

"It's something to do, Holly. Okay?"

Shawn was trying to get her mind off the taping session and what happened when they first arrived. She appreciated the effort, but doubted it would help.

"My original adoption papers said that Ruth Ann Miller was my birth mother. She was only seventeen at the time."

He moved around the desk, taking a seat behind it. "And your birth father's name?"

"George Foster. And that's all I know."

A fresh smile started in his eyes. "You know more than you think. So tell me again when and where you were born."

"Oh, all right." She released a bored sigh. "I— we were born on May 15, 1977, at Yellow-Rose Hospital in Houston, Texas. Satisfied?"

"And what was the name of that lawyer Bairn mentioned?"

"Verde. Walter R. Verde."

"Then your adoptive parents, the Harmons, never

went through an adoption agency in order to get you.''

"No, they've always just said that my adoption went through Mr. Verde's office."

He stopped talking and wrote something down. When he looked up again, tenderness lit up his entire face. "Did your parents know about Suzann?"

"They knew I had an identical twin sister, and they wanted to adopt her. But Mr. Verde said she wasn't available."

Shawn cocked his head to one side solicitously. "I wonder how someone as poor and uneducated as you said Suzann's mother was could afford to adopt a child?"

"Suzann thinks she knows the answer to that question. But of course, it's just speculation."

"And?"

"Suzann's adoptive father, Bob Condry, came from a wealthy Texas family who disowned him when he married her mother. Suzann's mother, Nancy Condry, might have thought she would be more acceptable to Bob's family if she produced a child. That's Suzann's theory, anyway. The trouble was, Nancy was unable to have children."

"So she got her rich husband to buy her a baby girl."

"That's what Suzann thinks."

"It's possible, I guess. Did the Condrys ever accept Suzann?"

"They only saw her briefly when they flew out to California for their son's funeral. Suzann thinks they must have been bitter, because they didn't even offer to help Suzann's mother pay for Bob's funeral expenses, much less anything else. Suzann said her mother had a hard time making ends meet until Suzann started raking in the money as a baby model and child actress.''

"Suzann's mother was a 'stage mom,' then?"

"Yes."

"Interesting." He tapped his pen on the desk. "Do you know anything else about Ruth Ann Miller—other than that she was an unwed, teenage mother?"

"Nothing," Holly said.

"How about George Foster?"

Holly shook her head, glancing toward the door. The crowd outside was getting louder. Shawn looked down. She assumed he was studying his notes.

He looked up again and smiled. "I'm sure Bairn will find your birth parents, sooner or later. If not, I will."

I will?

What did Shawn mean by that? She didn't think he should be trying to find her parents. He was taking on too much. She would have mentioned her concerns right then, but she kept thinking about that mob outside, wondering how they were going to make their way through it.

If that wasn't already more than she could handle, she had to give a speech shortly, and she'd never in her life felt more nervous nor more ill-prepared. Pulling this off would not be easy.

Shawn checked his watch. "It's time to go in, I guess."

Holly nodded. "I know."

He stood and gave her a big bear hug. Then he offered her his arm. "Just put on that smile of yours. You'll do fine, and stop worrying. The security guards here promised to clear the way for us."

Holly wasn't convinced.

The crowd of reporters she saw when they had first come in was abnormally large and growing larger. And she was expected to know most of the people waiting inside the banquet hall.

Oh, Shawn could introduce her to most of the doctors. That wasn't her problem. Representatives from the motion picture industry would be there too, and she didn't know any of them. She needed Mike's connections and knowledge of the Hollywood scene to make believable this speech she planned to give.

Mike had said he was coming later. He'd asked her to save him the seat next to hers. However, knowing Mike, she doubted he'd arrive any time soon. If he came at all. But strangely enough, Holly had come to be thankful for Mike's callous treatment of her. If he'd acted more responsibly about helping her, she'd never have met Shawn.

The security guards had managed to clear a path to the banquet hall. Two of them opened the big, double doors ahead of them. Holly expected a trumpet blast. At the least, she was prepared to hear her name announced at the end of a drumroll.

"Don't forget to shake hands with everybody, and smile," Shawn whispered. "I think that sounds like something Suzann would do, don't you?"

Holly had planned to do what he suggested. Still, it was kind of him to remind her.

She'd thought the mauve silk sheath and matching jacket she'd picked out that morning would be perfect for a banquet like this one. Now, after seeing everyone else in more formal attire, she wished she had worn something else.

The salad was served first. Mike still hadn't arrived.

"I guess Mike's not coming," she whispered to Shawn.

"Don't worry, he'll be here. I think your sister laid down the law."

Holly smiled to herself. Good for Suzann, she thought.

They had just been served the main course when Mike appeared from a side door. He smiled at Holly as if they were the best of friends.

"Sorry I'm late." He took the vacant chair to her left.

"*I'm* sorry you were too. You could have helped me with names and faces when I first came in."

"Don't worry." He placed his hand on her shoulder. "I can still do that."

"Fine." She brushed his hand away.

Shawn gazed at Holly and frowned. "Is my brother bothering you?"

"Not really. We're just talking."

After they finished eating, Shawn got up to introduce her. For the first time, Holly got to hear him speak publically. His voice was deep and commanding. Yet there was a warmth to it and a sense of joy. She positively adored and admired this man.

Holly expected him to talk about Suzann Condry.

But unknown to everyone else, Shawn talked about Holly Harmon. And he managed to do it in a way that would never cause suspicion.

In spite of Shawn's kind words and flattering remarks, Holly still wasn't sure she could give a convincing speech. Her knees shook, and she had a bad case of stage fright.

Yet after she actually stood behind the podium, at eye level with the crowd, a flash of valor she hadn't expected burst forth from deep within her. *That's the Lord,* she thought.

"It's a pleasure to be speaking on behalf of such a worthy cause," Holly said to the group. "Nothing is more important than children. They deserve the best medical care we can possibly give them, and that includes children in need."

When she finished speaking, Holly sat down to a round of applause.

"You sounded great," Shawn whispered.

"So did you," she replied, squeezing his hand. "So did you."

A larger group of reporters and cameramen waited outside as they attempted to leave the auditorium. The security guards she'd seen earlier tried their best to clear a path for them. This time, however, it didn't work. Holly felt like turning around and going back inside. She glanced back at Shawn and Mike, coming up behind her.

"What should we do?" she asked.

"Plow on through," Mike said. "That's what you-know-who would do."

She nodded. "You're right, of course."

"Don't believe him," Shawn shouted. "Stay right where you are."

Holly felt herself being pushed forward. Mike and Shawn were right beside her, one on each side, but seemed unable to keep up with her. The flow was too strong.

Someone put a microphone in her face. "Are you a Christian now, Miss Condry?"

Before she could answer, someone else said, "Are you and Greer Fraser back together?"

She opened her mouth to say "No comment." But by then another man was asking her a question. She had no idea what he said.

Someone grabbed hold of her arm, and she realized—to her relief—that it was Shawn. She didn't know how she made it inside the limo without being crushed to death.

On returning to the mansion, Holly found that Shawn had hired a crew of off-duty policemen to stand guard outside.

Holly spoke to her parents on the telephone several times. They were concerned after seeing all the media coverage of her dilemma on television, and they had wanted to come to California to see her. But Holly made them promise that they wouldn't.

Holly also had two long-distance telephone conversations with Suzann. Like Holly's parents, Suzann was concerned for Holly's safety. It wasn't easy to dissolve her sister's worries, but Holly had tried.

Later, Suzann recounted that after putting off singing a solo at church for so long, she finally sang "Amazing Grace" on the Sunday morning after

Thanksgiving. When Suzann described in glowing terms how Josh Gallagher accompanied her on the steel guitar, Holly wondered if Josh and Suzann were involved.

"I felt like I'd reached some sort of landmark," Suzann had said, "when I finally sang that song. Why, I'd put off singing in church since I got here. Pastor Jones was beginning to think I never would."

"What about Josh Gallagher? Did he think the same thing?"

"No," Suzann said. "Josh always knew I intended to sing. The question was always when."

Holly thought her sister had sounded hopeful when she talked about Josh Gallagher. But later, when their conversation turned to other areas, Suzann's voice had sounded hollow—as if she was desperately afraid or was hiding something.

Had something important occurred that Suzann wasn't telling? Was Suzann only pretending to be up-beat to keep from revealing her true feelings?

"That reminds me," Suzann said, cutting into her thoughts. "Did I mention that Dexter Simpson offered me a job?"

"Job? What job?"

"On Saturday I received a sermon that Dexter had promised to send me, along with a letter. He offered me a job, teaching drama to the young people at his church in Dallas."

"Are you interested?" Holly asked.

"Are you kidding? Not in a million years."

"Maybe you should consider it. You might not like slipping back into the fishbowl."

"At the end of the six months, when this is really over, I'll love living in a fishbowl again."

Holly disagreed with her sister. However, she let the subject drop.

"You were about to tell me what happened on Thanksgiving Day," Holly said, "and why you came back early."

"I was not."

"Yes, you were. Twins know these things."

"Sometimes," Suzann said, "I think you know me better than I know myself."

"I know." Holly laughed.

What had surprised Holly the most about their conversation was what happened next. Suzann had asked Holly some biblical questions. When Holly had finally answered all the questions, Suzann had gone on to question her about faith and God.

Was Suzann on the verge of inviting the Lord into her life?

Maybe. Time would tell. In the meantime, Holly intended to pray like crazy.

On the first Tuesday afternoon after Thanksgiving, Greer Fraser sent Holly a basket of yellow roses. It was amazing that the flowers got through the army of reporters that constantly stood guard outside Suzann's front door.

The mansion was literally under siege with reporters standing in flower beds, under bushes, and peering out from nearby houses with their zoom-lenses pointing toward the Condry mansion. Later, as Holly looked out an upstairs window, she saw Greer's dark green sports car pull to a stop out front.

Reporters and photographers clustered around his car the way they had swarmed around the mansion since Holly returned from the fund-raiser. She worried that Greer might never make it inside.

Holly received Greer in the Blue Room, determined to pretend that the goings-on outside were nothing unusual.

"I do appreciate the flowers you sent," Holly said woodenly. "But I really can't understand why you bothered when we split months ago."

"I like the new you." He pushed up the long sleeves of his green sweater that just happened to match his eyes. "That's why."

"What new me?"

"The one I saw at the opening and on television this morning."

"What do you mean—television?"

"I'm talking about that commercial you made to raise money for Crystal-Bay Children's Hospital. Everybody's talking about how dewy-fresh you seemed, and that's a plus."

"Well, at least they're taking notice for a good cause. The Children's Hospital is the point, though. Not how I look."

"You should be thankful for the publicity," he said. "It will do wonders for your career."

"Are you hoping it will do wonders for yours too?"

He leveled a finger at her jokingly. A dimpled grin appeared. "You got me there." He winked. "I want to start seeing you again, Sue. When will you let me take you to dinner?"

"We'll see." Holly looked down at the floor the way she'd seen Suzann do in numerous movies. She could only hope her lowered lashes hid her innocence.

"You know—" a smile started in his eyes and spread "—it's almost like you're a completely different person." His voice took on provocative overtones. "And I find the *new* you intensely exciting." He moved to the couch and sat down beside her. "You're incredible, really."

"I merely took off a few pounds. That's all."

"Did you have a face lift too?"

"A what?" Holly's cheeks and her temper heated up. "No."

"Sorry, but you do look...different somehow." Greer shrugged. "How should I put this? You look the same, only better, and I love that winsome stare. You should have added that years ago. And if you did engage in a little face and body repair, who cares? The overall effect is great. The reporters are raving about how young and innocent you look these days. And I think visiting that church was a stroke of genius."

Holly's body grew rigid again, straining to hear what he might say next. No matter what, Holly was not going to let Greer or anybody else make fun of Shawn's church or the God she served.

"Why, the publicity those visits to the church are creating alone makes me downright jealous," Greer said. "In fact, I'm considering the church angle myself. Perhaps we should join forces and go together next Sunday? I'm game if you are."

"What would you say if I told you I'm already a Christian?" she asked.

He laughed.

"Really, Greer, I'm a Christian now. Trust me on this. And I wanted you to be the first to know that I plan to join the church I've been attending."

He frowned as if he was measuring her words. Then a slow smile materialized.

"You really had me going there for a minute," he said, "and you're an even better actress than I thought. If you think pretending to join a church will help get your name in the newspapers again, I say go for it. I just wish I'd thought of the idea first."

He reached into the briefcase he'd brought along, pulling out a stack of tabloid newspapers.

"I thought you probably hadn't been out much, with the press watching your every move," he said. "I figured you might enjoy reading these." He handed the newspapers to Holly. "By the way, did you know you're the queen of the tabloids this week? Why, your beautiful face is everywhere."

Holly was not impressed.

"I don't know who is managing your career," he said, "but—"

God's managing my life, thank you very much, she thought.

"Anyway," he continued, "if it's Mike, he's doing a magnificent job. My hat goes off to the man."

Greer had his mind made up. There was no point in pushing the issue further. He could believe whatever he liked. Holly was going to join Shawn's church as soon as she found the fortitude to face those reporters again.

Greer rose from his chair. "Well, I guess I'll be going."

Holly walked Greer to the door. He moved toward her, as if he was about to kiss her goodbye, but Holly nimbly stepped out of his reach.

"I'll be in touch," Greer promised as he left.

Holly waved goodbye, saying nothing.

When Greer had gone, Holly reached for the newspapers he'd left behind. Looking down at the first headline, she saw the name *Suzann* in big letters: Has Suzann Condry Found God? She flipped to the next one: Did God Bring Suzann and Greer Back Together?

Holly hated all the tabloid stories because they were based on lies and half-truths concocted to sell newspapers. She knew of unlikely people who had found God and got saved. The Lord brought couples together too, restored marriages and families, and healed sickness and disease.

However, Holly wished there was some way she could discredit stories like the ones in the tabloids. She could refuse to be interviewed by tabloid reporters, of course, and she planned to do that. But getting them to stop taking her picture would be harder.

Later that same afternoon, Shawn arrived at the mansion. Since he reached the door rather quickly, Holly assumed that he told the press that he was Suzann's doctor and needed to go inside immediately. Watching from her bedroom window upstairs again,

Holly realized she had a terrible headache. No wonder, with all that was going on.

The police had tried to break up the crowd of reporters earlier. So far, they hadn't been successful.

Holly met Shawn at the foot of the stairs. He hugged her, and she hugged him back. Then he placed a quick kiss on her cheek.

She hadn't intended to pull away, but sharp pains shot through her head with every movement she made: she needed to take a couple of aspirin before her headache got worse. A perplexed expression flashed across Shawn's face.

"Why don't we go into the Blue Room for an early supper?" she suggested. "I'll have Bates bring in some sandwiches."

"Sure," he said. "That'll be—that'll be great."

"And forgive me if I seem slightly weird today." Holly pressed her fingertips to her forehead. "I have a terrible headache."

Shawn nodded, then followed her inside.

"I'm closing the curtains," she said, "to block out the circus outside."

A few minutes later, Bates brought in the sandwiches.

"How are you surviving all this?" Shawn took a bite of his sandwich, placing the rest back on his plate. "It can't be easy, being held captive by the press day and night."

"I'm managing."

"I'm not so sure." He hesitated as if in deep thought. "I think you should plan to leave the mansion as soon as we can arrange it."

"Where would you suggest I go?" she asked. "Oak Valley, Texas, is a little crowded right now."

"I talked to Suzann early this morning, and she has it all worked out."

Holly blinked. "Really?"

"She owns a hideaway in Alameda, California, that almost nobody knows about. The house fronts on a canal that angles off San Francisco Bay. She says you're going to love living there."

"Just because we're twins doesn't mean I always like what my sister does." Holly pressed her fingers to her forehead again.

She'd forgotten to have Bates send in the aspirins. Her headache was getting worse.

"By the way, with the press waiting outside," she said, "how would I get out of here?"

"All the details haven't been worked out yet." Shawn went over and stood behind Holly's chair. "But they will be soon."

Shawn rubbed her neck and shoulders with the palms of his hands. She closed her eyes, feeling stress pour out of her.

"I think you should prepare to leave as soon as possible," he said.

Chapter Twelve

Suzann woke up with her stomach tied in knots. She thought she knew why.

Play practice for the Christmas program began right after school on Monday. Suzann deliberately scheduled all the practice sessions during the daylight hours. However, today, Wednesday, choir practice met at night after church. She would be driving home alone after dark.

She'd spent more time than she probably should have, thinking about the man in the green suit. At the police station in San Antonio, Officer Edwards had suggested counseling, insisting that attacks like hers warranted it.

The truth was that the press paid big bucks for stories about celebrities. Counselors would be tempted to tell all.

I can do this, Suzann told herself. I can get in my car and drive on home tonight after choir practice.

By nightfall, all her good intentions disappeared.

Suzann stiffened, looking out the choir room's upstairs window. The parking lot glowed with soft, yellow lights. Sure, the church had spent a great deal of money on a new lighting system, but Suzann wanted more. She wanted the church parking lot *super* lighted, not edged in shadows and patched with darkness.

Okay, Heavenly Father, this is Suzann, requesting special favors. I need to get out to that parking lot safely. Then I need to drive home and get inside without having a panic attack. Please answer this prayer because I'm really, really scared. Amen.

When she finished praying, Suzann realized two things. Prayer helped calm her nerves. And she wasn't sophisticated anymore. She wondered if she'd ever been so.

She glanced out the window again. Hers was the only car she could see from her vantage point. This was not encouraging.

In hindsight, she should have hurried. Instead, she stood around the choir room, talking with fellow choir members, drinking hot coffee, and hoping somebody would offer to follow her home. When she left, briefly, to go to the rest room, she returned to an empty room.

She supposed she should just trek out to the parking lot and hope for the best. What could happen to her in a church parking lot? Memories of the church in San Antonio caused her heart to pump a little faster.

The overhead lights blinked on and off. Her throat contracted. Indisputably, this was a warning. The janitor, Mr. Turner, was checking to make sure everybody was out of the building before he turned off all the lights.

It was comforting to know somebody else was still inside. Just not comforting enough.

She took a step toward the door. A board creaked in the hallway outside.

Suzann's slender body shook all over. "Is somebody there?"

There was no reply.

She felt panic mounting. Could the sound she heard have been the old building settling down for the night? Yes, that had to be it.

So why couldn't she accept that? Why couldn't she just walk down those stairs and out onto the parking lot the way all the other choir members had done?

The lights blinked on and off again. Warning number two. She had to go now or chance spending the night inside.

The hallway outside looked dark, scary. The stairway would be even darker.

I can do this, Lord.

If only she believed that.

Suzann moved out into the hallway, strode toward the stairs at a brisk pace. Her pulse raced.

At the landing, halfway down, the stairway took a sharp turn to the left. She wouldn't be able to see what lay ahead until she made that turn.

She released a deep breath and descended the stairs, two at a time. Then she slipped.

Suzann felt herself falling forward. Her heart skipped several beats as she groped for the wooden railing. Then she just stood there, shaking from head to toe and wondering if she had the courage to try again.

Holly had given her a Bible scripture at the cabin to use at times like this. If only she could remember it.

She started down again, creeping slowly and taking one step at a time.

She reached the landing, finally. Now the turn. Looking down from the landing, all she saw was blackness. Suzann shivered, then reminded herself to be brave.

Once she reached the hallway on the ground floor, she would only be about fifteen feet from the parking lot. But she wouldn't think about the parking lot now. First things first.

Suzann stopped, squinting up at the ceiling just above her head. Both bulbs were out. No wonder it was so dark.

Lovely.

Peering down from the landing, the stairway looked menacing. She should have been able to see the door leading to the parking lot, but she couldn't see a thing.

The lights blinked again. Then darkness.

"Help!" she called out. "I'm still in here."

Black silence wrapped around her like a cloak. Her breath compacted.

Cautiously, she crept downward. She still couldn't see anything.

A step creaked behind her. Suzann halted, paralyzed. Was someone following her?

She finally reached the bottom of the stairs. All she

needed to do now was make a run for the door and hope she was running in the right direction. She raced forward blindly.

Suddenly Suzann bumped into something—or someone—hard. Fear froze her as arms reached around her. Someone held her so tightly that she could scarcely breathe.

"Help!" she shouted.

"Holly? Is that you?"

Relief flooded her. It was Josh. Suzann fell against his shoulder, sobbing her thanks. But my name's Suzann, she thought.

"What are you doing here?" he asked.

She didn't have the strength to reply. She just kept holding him and letting him hold her.

Josh hadn't attended choir practice. Someone in the choir had said Brother Josh had to make a hospital visit. Suzann hadn't known that he returned or that he was in the building.

She was just glad he was.

"I stopped by the church office to pick up some papers," Josh said, "and Mr. Turner asked me to lock up for him. But I thought everybody was out of the building a long time ago."

Suzann wanted to ask if he had heard her call out. She wanted to ask if he would mind driving her home. She wanted to say a lot of things. She was just too upset to open her mouth.

"You're trembling," he said. "You poor thing, you must have been frightened in there all alone."

"I was," she said. "Would you mind holding me a little longer, please?"

He chuckled under his breath. "I'll give it my best shot."

And then he kissed her.

Joy. Release. Tenderness. It wasn't a long kiss. Actually it was over almost before it began. Yet a kind of sweet excitement still rippled through her.

Josh turned her to the side, then, and put his arm around her shoulders. She assumed that he was aiming her toward the exit door. And that was fine with Suzann.

"I'm going to drive you home," he said.

"What about your truck?"

"I'll walk back here and get it later."

"You really don't mind?"

"Mind? I'd consider it an honor."

She knew that it was wrong to let him walk back to the parking lot in the dark like that. At the same time, she wanted him to be there for her.

Frankly, she hoped he'd come inside and stay until she calmed down. The thought of being alone terrified her.

When they arrived at her apartment, Josh walked her all the way to her door. She shivered, thinking how frightened she was going to be when he left her.

"You're still shaking," he said.

"I'm okay." Why did I say that? she chided herself. I'm not okay, not at all.

"Why don't you let me phone one of the women of the church to come over here and spend the night with you?"

"That's not necessary." But please do it anyway, she pleaded silently.

"The expression on your face says that it *is* necessary." He reached for her purse, then fished for her apartment key. "I could phone Kate and ask her to come over."

Not Kate, she thought.

Suzann still struggled with Kate's confession about her love for Josh. On one hand, Suzann felt sorry for her; on the other, she was upset that Kate hadn't been honest about her feelings sooner. A kind gesture on Kate's part could make Suzann feel guilty for not pardoning her.

"Unless you'd rather have someone else," he added.

"It would be an imposition to ask anyone."

"Kate won't mind."

Suzann didn't argue. Josh was right. She didn't want to spend the night alone.

Josh pulled Suzann down beside him on the couch. "I'll phone Kate. Then I'll wait until she gets here."

His nearness warmed her. Suzann found herself snuggling even closer. He patted the back of her head. Then he reached for the phone and dialed the number. When Kate answered he explained what happened at the church earlier that evening. Then asked her to come over to Suzann's and spend the night.

Kate must have said yes. Josh smiled and said, "Thanks. I'll see you in a few minutes."

When Josh hung up the phone, he gazed deeply into Suzann's eyes.

"Kate's coming then?" Suzann asked.

He nodded, taking her in his arms again. "She'll be right over." Josh touched her forehead, brushing back a lock of her long hair. "I love to hold you," he said.

I love it when you hold me, she thought.

"Right now, I'd like to kiss you." His voice held an emotional undercurrent that Suzann found both tender and exciting. "And kiss you…and kiss you…and kiss you," he added. "You probably wouldn't like that, would you?"

Try me, she thought.

"But I'd like it," he said. "And do you know why?"

She gazed up at him, shaking her head, pretending she'd never had such desires. Simulating an innocence she didn't possess.

"I know this is hard for someone like you to understand," he said, "but I'm attracted to you—in every way possible. Can you understand what I'm saying?"

If he only knew.

"Is it possible that by some miracle you might feel the same way about me?"

I feel the things you're feeling, she thought, and I'm trying as hard as I can not to. Please help me to not love you.

Yet she knew in her heart that it was much too late. She loved Josh Gallagher. She would never love another man as long as she lived.

But she hadn't replied to any of his questions.

All at once, he pulled away. She'd hurt him again. The wounded expression on his face confirmed it. If only she could tell him how she really felt.

Suzann longed to reach out to Josh. She wanted to

tell him she loved him, hold him in her arms, and have him hold her in return. But that was out of the question. He was in love with Holly Harmon. And *she*—Suzann—was a liar and an impostor.

"I've embarrassed you," he said. "I've said too much. This was not the right time at all. You've had such a scare tonight. I should have waited—taken this slow and easy—given you more time."

The tender look on his face called out to her, captured her. Even if she'd wanted to look away, it would have been impossible to manage.

Slowly, she felt her face moving toward his. Her gaze settled on his lips. He was about to kiss her again. She felt unable to move, to speak, to breath.

Slowly, his mouth found hers.

Their kiss said everything she'd been waiting to hear—everything she'd been hoping to say and more. If Josh hadn't known how she felt about him before, he would know now. Another kiss began before the first one had really ended.

There was a knock at the door.

Josh pulled away first and got to his feet. "That'll be Kate."

"Yes." Suzann sat up and ran her hands through her hair.

"Shall I get the door?" he asked.

"Please."

Josh took a deep breath and opened the door. Kate came in carrying the suitcase Suzann had left at the ranch on Thanksgiving Day.

She set the suitcase on the floor by the door. "Well, here I am," she announced brightly. If she suspected that she'd interrupted a romantic moment between Josh and Suzann, she didn't let on. "How are you feeling, Holly?"

"Much better," Suzann said. "Thanks for coming over." Suzann got up off the couch and headed for the kitchen. "Coffee, anyone?" she asked over her shoulder.

"None for me," Josh and Kate said together.

Suzann turned back. "Then I don't want coffee, either." Inwardly, she still trembled from Josh's kiss. But she tried hard to seem calm.

Suzann sat down on the couch beside Kate. As an afterthought, she gestured toward the rocker in the hope that Josh would take that chair. After what happened when Kate first came in, she wanted him as far from her as possible.

Embarrassment was a new emotion for Suzann. She didn't know how to handle it yet.

"No chair for me, thanks," Josh said. "I've gotta go."

Suzann nodded, and he left almost immediately.

Suzann turned to Kate. "You can't know how much I appreciate you coming over like this. I'm a basket case after what happened at the church tonight."

"You must have been terrified."

"I was."

Suzann couldn't think of anything else to say. She didn't feel like talking more about her frightening experience. "You take my bed tonight, Kate." Suzann patted the couch. "I'll sleep right here."

"No way. I'm not going to take your bed."

"Please do. I feel bad enough dragging you out of your own place tonight. I'd sleep on the floor if I had to rather than stay here alone all night."

Kate took hold of Suzann's hand. "Let's talk first. It might help."

Suzann recoiled, pondering what Kate might want to discuss. She assumed Kate wanted to talk about Josh or bring up what happened on Thanksgiving. Suzann wasn't in the mood to address either of those topics.

"I want to talk about your fears," Kate said. "I know you must have plenty after what happened that day in San Antonio. And now this."

Suzann relaxed slightly. "Where should we begin?"

"This is your call."

Suzann sensed that she needed to trust and even forgive Kate completely, and she truly wanted to do that. She just didn't know how.

Until she had moved to Oak Valley, forgiveness was never an option for Suzann. Never mind trust. Nobody she knew ever truly forgave anybody. They merely said they forgave while holding on to all the bitterness. They never trusted anyone, or let down their defenses to be totally honest—and vulnerable. But Pastor Jones had said that true forgiveness dissolved hate and bitterness. And honesty could not exist in a relationship without trust.

A nudge to go ahead and forgive Kate came from— She didn't know where.

Somehow she knew that if she ever did learn to forgive, she would be able to put down a heavy burden. A burden she'd been carrying around since childhood.

Boldly, Suzann shared her fears with Kate Devlon. She began with a traumatic event that happened during her childhood when, while working at a movie set, she was locked in a dark storage room by Dexter Quin. Since Kate still believed she was Holly, Suzann took care to relate only the important details of the story. But while talking about her memories, Suzann suddenly realized that Dexter had been suffering from the pressure of being a child star just as much as she had.

Kate listened intently, then offered some helpful suggestions for overcoming her fear.

Most of what Kate said was merely common sense. What impressed Suzann the most, however, was Kate's apparent faith in God, plus her knowledge of Scripture. Suzann planned to write down as many of the Bible Scriptures as she could remember.

By the time they finished their talk, Suzann felt a lot better and very grateful to Kate. Kate wasn't perfect, but she was a true Christian. Her help during Suzann's time of need proved that.

Suzann slept on the couch that night. But not before she'd underlined the Scriptures Kate gave her in Holly's Bible.

Tomorrow, she would buy a Bible of her own.

Chapter Thirteen

Holly had thought Shawn's plan to get her safely out of the mansion was doomed to failure. How could they possibly escape with the press assembled outside?

The police ran off the mob of reporters several times, but they always returned. Then on Friday, Shawn's entire scenario played out perfectly right before her eyes. They were able to leave her sister's beautiful estate.

Posing as furniture movers, the security guards Suzann hired pretended to leave new furniture at the mansion while Holly and Shawn hid in their empty truck. Later the guards managed to slip the furniture truck past the legions of reporters.

While Holly and Shawn waited in the back of the truck, the guards drove them to the parking garage where Shawn left his van. From there, they headed north on the interstate. They hoped to reach Suzann's waterfront hideaway in Alameda by supper time.

Holly had put all her worries and concerns on the back burner during the bumpy ride in the furniture truck. Now that they were in the van, she attempted to make some sense of her relationship with Shawn McDowell.

Shawn had been her knight in shining armor when she first arrived in California. She didn't know what she would have done without him. Later, he became her best friend, and then her big brother.

The trouble was, Holly was in love with Shawn. She kept praying that he would declare his love for her, but he never did. Sometimes, she was almost positive he had serious feelings for her. Then she'd come back down to earth and recognize that she mustn't read any special meaning into his fond gazes, or even warm hugs. Surely, if he thought of her as more than a friend he would have let her know by now. Besides, she was soon returning to Oak Valley, while he needed to stay here in California.

Feeling the way she did about him, she determined that she should separate herself from Shawn before he broke her heart.

She'd spent time considering how to do that. As a Christian, she knew she should be kind. Finally, she decided to make a clean break and tell Shawn outright that she didn't think they should see each other anymore.

She'd searched for the proper time. The long drive to Alameda seemed perfect—if she had the nerve to do it.

Shawn felt Holly watching him from the passenger seat. Turning, he smiled. "How's it going?"

"Frankly, I've been feeling guilty," Holly said. "I think you've spent entirely too much time away from your practice because of me."

"I don't mind."

"I know, and you've been an angel to help out the way you have. But it simply isn't fair to you."

Shawn pensively cocked his head to one side. "Is there something more to this?"

"I want things to be different once I'm settled in the house in Alameda."

"Different? How?"

"I think it would be unwise to pretend I'm Suzann Condry there. That would only attract the press. So I've decided to be somebody completely different— not Suzann Condry and not Holly Harmon. Just somebody different."

Shawn tensed. What was she saying? And why did he have the feeling he was about to be dumped?

"I've been like a bird with a broken wing that you've had to nurse back to health," Holly said. "But my wing's healed now."

Was she preparing to fly away? You could always marry me. He cleared his throat. "Did it ever occur to you that I might *like* treating broken wings?"

"Of course you do. You're a doctor. That's what doctors do. But treating the same patient for the same problem has to seem tiresome sooner or later."

Never, when it's you.

"And I really can't impose on you any longer," she said.

He had to give her credit. Women had broken up

with him previously, but he'd never been dumped more gently or more kindly in his entire life.

"You're a wonderful person and a wonderful friend," she said. "I've felt grateful to know you, honestly."

Had he heard a quiver in her voice? Perhaps the start of a sob? Or was that just wishful thinking?

"I always felt that helping me was a ministry for you," she said.

"It is."

Shawn coughed, then cleared his throat again. He had to come up with some way to keep their relationship in one piece until he found a way to fix it.

Until he met Holly, Shawn thought all beautiful women were like Tina, the woman who had broken his heart. Sure, he'd said he intended to break up with Holly before she beat him to the punch, but that was just an internal dialogue that played in his head sometimes. A way of protecting his feelings, he realized. He'd never seriously considered pushing Holly out of his life. Why, he'd do anything to keep them together.

It was unlikely that Beauty would want to share her life with an ordinary guy like Shawn McDowell. But he had to find out for sure before he walked away for the last time.

"You see," he said, "I've felt from the first day I met you that my mission was to help you carry out yours."

She grew silent. He assumed she was composing a reply.

"So, when do you think that mission of yours might be completed?" she asked.

"After I know you're safe and your birth parents have been found."

"That's really very noble of you, Shawn. But it isn't fair. I mean, finding my birth parents could take months, even years. Surely you're not prepared to invest that much time in something like this. Besides, Mr. Bairn is looking for my birth parents as we speak."

"Not anymore." He increased his speed and pulled in behind a big eighteen-wheeler. "Suzann had Mike fire Bairn last night."

A startled look surfaced. "Why?"

"We think Bairn was selling information about you and Suzann to a tabloid newspaper."

"Can you prove it?"

"I'm close." The eighteen-wheeler switched to another lane. Shawn accelerated. "With Mike's blessing, I hired another detective. I've had Bairn under surveillance for several weeks. I happen to think he's a crook. So I let Bairn know in no uncertain terms that he could be fired from his job at the detective agency. Then I gave him an offer he couldn't refuse. Give me all the information he's gathered so far or—"

"Lose his job at the agency."

"Precisely."

Holly appeared to be in deep thought.

"Since I found out what Bairn was doing," Shawn said, "I've been searching for your birth parents on my own. I've already got some pretty good leads."

"What leads?"

"Visiting your birth mother's sister, for starters."

"You've located my—my aunt?"

"Yeah. We'll be visiting her tomorrow."

"That's wonderful news." She reached over and gave Shawn a spontaneous hug. Then she looked as if she regretted doing it—as if she'd done something wrong. "My, you've been busy, haven't you? How did you manage to find her?"

"Bairn found her. He just wasn't planning to tell anybody about it—except the tabloid press, of course."

"Do the tabloids know about my aunt?"

"I don't think so, but it's possible, I guess."

"We better hurry then if we expect to find my parents before the press do." She still gazed at Shawn as if she had questions she wanted answered. "Is that all you know about this?"

He paused. "Not entirely. Your sister phoned me last night."

"Suzann?"

He nodded. "It seems she and Pastor Gallagher were having coffee at a café after church. And someone snapped a picture of them at their table. Suzann thinks it was a reporter."

"Then it's only a matter of time before this whole thing blows up in our faces."

"I think you might be right."

Several tabloid newspapers were stacked on the dashboard of Shawn's van. Holly reached for them, then flipped through the stack. He already had the headlines memorized.

"Is Suzann Condry a Religious Fanatic? Has the

Real Suzann Condry Disappeared? Is an Alien Living in Suzann Condry's Body?''

"Well," Shawn asked, "what do you think?"

"These people are crazy."

He nodded, looking down the road ahead. He had no idea what Holly was thinking or planning. However, he had a nagging feeling that it was not good news as far as he was concerned.

Holly hadn't realized they had reached Alameda until Shawn turned down a quiet street in an older neighborhood. As she looked on, he slowed. Then he appeared to study the number over the door of a little white, wooden house, off to their left.

"That's it," he said. "1601."

An impressive open stairway led from the entry down to the other two levels of the house, finally reaching the living room with its eighteen-foot ceiling.

Sliding glass doors on three sides looked out from the huge room, leading directly to a private dock. A combination of antiques and a nautical decor appealed to Holly's tastes perfectly.

Shawn put down her suitcases. "Think you're going to like it here?"

"Who wouldn't?"

Shawn had been somber and reflective since their discussion earlier. Holly had felt depressed. Seeing the Alameda house lifted her spirits. When she saw Shawn's halfhearted grin, she assumed his mood had improved too.

He moved to the sliding glass doors. "Can you believe this view?"

"I've never lived so near saltwater before. Why, you can actually smell it, can't you?"

He opened the glass door and took a deep breath. "Sure can. Want to go exploring?"

She nodded, then followed him out onto the wooden deck. A small motorboat was tied to a pier no more than thirty feet from the back of the house.

"What a beautiful place," she said, taking in the view. "It truly is a special hideaway."

"Yes, it is special," Shawn agreed. "I know you'll want to unpack now and rest. But one of these days I want us to take the boat out to Fisherman's Wharf. I hear the food there is great."

Us? She'd thought their relationship was winding down. Yet he was still talking about plans for the future.

Lord, You know I love Shawn McDowell and want to marry him. Nevertheless, not my will but Thy will be done.

She glanced back at Shawn, planning to tell him that taking a ride in a small boat all the way to San Francisco seemed a little much. Then her stomach reminded her that she hadn't eaten for hours.

"I'm starved," she said.

"I'll go get take-out then. I'll try to find a video store and rent a movie to watch tonight, if you like."

"I assumed you'd be driving back to Burbank."

"I'm taking a week off and will be staying at a motel here in Alameda."

Shawn was full of surprises. Holly still wasn't convinced that he grasped the message she was trying to send him. However, if he planned to be in the city for an entire week, she would have plenty of opportunities to make him understand.

"So what do you think?" he asked.

"I think take-out and a movie sounds great."

After a supper of hamburgers and fries, they settled on the couch to watch the video. It was a spy movie, and one Holly was eager to see.

Shawn sat down on the couch first. When Holly joined him there a few minutes later, she moved way down to the other end. During the first part of the movie, he kept inching her way. By the time the story put her on the edge of her seat, he was right beside her.

"This movie's supposed to be scary." He grinned impishly, then laced his hand with hers. "You might need moral support."

She had to smile. Later, when he put his arm around her and that same mischievous expression returned, she found it impossible to hold in a laugh. When she finally did laugh, he laughed too, and his arm curved around her shoulder.

The movie flashed to the villain. He was sneaking up on the hero, who had just entered a dark room.

Shawn pulled her body close.

Being in his arms felt so right and comforting that she found herself snuggling even closer. Later still, she put her head on his shoulder.

At the end of the movie, when the credits were

rolling, he turned her toward him, held her face with his hands, and kissed her.

A thrill simmered through her. Momentarily, all thoughts of ending their relationship evaporated.

He held her close then, outlining her chin with his thumb. Her heart sang for joy.

He loves me, she thought, and I love him.

Holly waited for Shawn to say the words she longed to hear. Yet no words came.

Instead, he got up and headed for the kitchen. "I'm going to get myself another cola. Would you like one too?"

Her heart compressed. Was that all their first real kiss had meant to him? Had it merely invoked a desire for a cold drink?

"Hey," he called from the kitchen, "do you want one or not?"

"No, I think I'll pass on that. I probably need to turn in early tonight. Any more cola might keep me awake."

Before he left for the motel, Shawn promised to stop by the next morning and take her on a long drive. They would also be visiting her aunt. So Holly agreed to go in spite of her misgivings.

Shawn appeared at her door early Saturday morning.

"I know you'll need groceries and other supplies," he said. "So I thought you could buy the things you need while we're out."

"That's thoughtful of you."

He was friendly and lighthearted. Had that kiss

canceled out her "goodbye forever" speech? Or had it merely gone in one ear and out the other?

"I really appreciate all the help you're giving me," she said. "But what about your practice?"

"I haven't had a vacation in years. My partner at the clinic is only too willing to fill in."

"But what about weekend duty at the hospital? Aren't you supposed to be there?"

"Until I met you, I spent almost every weekend at the hospital while my married colleagues spent time with their families. I have some free weekends stacked up that I plan to use until they're gone."

"I see."

He wasn't making it easy to break this off. Was there a simple way? If so, she hadn't found it.

"Since you seem to have everything mapped out anyway," she said, "what are our plans for today?"

"I'm sorry, Holly. I never intended to control you. I just want to help out a very nice Christian lady."

Then why don't you fall in love with me? she wondered. That would be a very nice thing to do.

"You still haven't told me where we're going this morning," she said.

"I thought we'd take the drawbridge to Oakland. From there, we'd drive into the hills around Berkeley for a while and look around. Then take the Bay Bridge to San Francisco, have an early lunch on Fisherman's Wharf, and do a little shopping."

"And then?"

"We're expected at Mrs. Frances Miller Reagan's home at three this afternoon."

"That would be my aunt. Does this mean you also know where to find my birth parents?"

"Afraid not, but I'm working on it." He hesitated. "Let's just say that I think I know how to find out that information. Your aunt may know more than she was willing to say over the telephone."

They arrived at Mrs. Reagan's house right on time. The elderly widow seemed extremely nervous.

Holly hoped that her aunt wouldn't connect her with Suzann Condry until she got to know her. Without makeup and wearing glasses, Holly thought she looked like a church librarian again.

"You're Ruthie's child," Mrs. Reagan said. "She was my baby sister, you know."

Holly tensed. "Was?"

Mrs. Reagan wiped a tear from her gray eyes. "Ruthie's gone to Heaven."

Holly's heart skipped a beat. "You mean my mother is dead?"

"Since she was nineteen years old."

Holly covered her mouth with her right hand, hoping to muffle any cries that might try to escape. "How—how did she die?"

"A car accident. She was driving alone, late at night. A terrible storm, I remember. She should've pulled over and stopped until the storm passed. But she'd been distracted, depressed. Not thinking very clearly since she gave her babies up for adoption. It broke her heart, you see. And she never got over it."

"I'm a Christian," Holly said, "and I've always hoped that my real mother was saved too."

"She was."

Holly felt a burst of hope. "Really?"

"Oh, my, yes. She repented mightily for her mistakes. I do know your father was the only man she'd ever loved, and she did love him truly."

"I guess I wondered about that," Holly admitted. "Why didn't they marry?"

Mrs. Reagan was seated on a dusty, brown couch. When she saw a glimmer of expectation on Holly's face, Mrs. Reagan motioned for Holly to sit down beside her.

"Your father was engaged to another woman when he met and fell in love with Ruthie. He promised to come back to her when he was free, but by the time he'd sorted out his life, it was too late."

"How sad," Holly said. "But I'm glad to hear my mother was saved. My family and I have prayed for my birth parents all my life. It's a blessing to know she had faith."

"Well, those prayers must have done some good, don't you think?"

"Yes, ma'am, I sure do."

"Would you mind calling me Aunt Frances, honey? It appears that you and your sister are the only kinfolk I have left in this world."

Suzann hugged her aunt for the first time. "I'd love to call you Aunt Frances, and I think my sister will too."

"Pardon me, ma'am," Shawn put in, "but would you happen to know how to get hold of Holly's birth father, George Foster?"

"Well, I don't know where he lives," Mrs. Reagan

said. "But I do know he's about to retire from the United States Navy.

"And he'll be tickled to see you," Aunt Frances continued. "He was aboard ship when you girls were born. Ruthie never told him she was expecting. When he came back and I told him she died, I never told him he had two daughters somewhere."

"Why not?" Holly asked.

"I don't know." Aunt Frances glanced away briefly. "It just seemed too cruel, I guess. There was no way on God's earth he could hope to get either one of you back. He was broken-hearted enough over losing Ruthie. So I guess I just thought it was better that he not know how much more he'd lost."

Holly disagreed with her aunt's conclusions. Who was Aunt Frances to make such an important decision? However, she kept her opinions to herself.

After they were back in Shawn's van again, Holly gazed up at him and smiled. "Thank you for today, Shawn," she said, "and for finding my aunt for me. I wish my mother was still alive, but it's great to know that someday I'll get to meet her in Heaven."

"Knowing that makes me happy too," Shawn said. "And who knows? Maybe we'll find out that your dad is saved too. At the least we'll find him. That's a promise."

Holly and Shawn attended church the next morning in Alameda. Afterward, he took her out to lunch. But nothing had changed. They were simply living in a new setting.

Holly still wanted Shawn out of her life. Seeing

him daily when she knew he didn't love her was too distressing to handle anymore.

She talked to Suzann on the telephone several times. However, she didn't share her thoughts and feelings. Suzann didn't share much, either. Holly still thought Suzann was going through something traumatic, but she had no idea what it might be.

On Wednesday Shawn arrived at her door with a triumphant expression on his face. Somehow, she knew he'd found her birth father.

"You found him," she exclaimed, "didn't you?"

"Yep. Are you ready to meet him?"

"I've been waiting all my life."

She needed to remind Shawn that they had reached that point in their relationship that they had talked about earlier. After she visited with her father, she and Shawn must go their separate ways.

Just thinking about such a declaration broke her heart. Maybe it would even be painful for Shawn.

She needed to phone her father and tell him who she was before she went to see him. It wouldn't be right merely to show up on his doorstep.

The drive to George Foster's house seemed to take forever. Holly should have been thinking about their first meeting. Instead, her thoughts returned again and again to Shawn and what she must say to him.

Would he miss her? Or would he be glad to have the whole thing over and done with? She knew *she* would be devastated.

Holly never really knew when they left Alameda and reached the city limits of Hayward, California.

To her, the entire area was just one urban sprawl. Or maybe it was because her thoughts were elsewhere.

George Foster's house was small. She wondered if he'd ever married—if he had other children. She hoped to get answers to all her questions. Anything to stop thinking about Shawn.

Holly could only imagine what George must have thought when she phoned him and introduced herself. How do you tell a man he has two grown daughters and that they are identical twins? The fact that Suzann was a movie star must have seemed even more unbelievable to him.

The first thing she noticed when he opened the door was a thick mass of reddish hair streaked with gray. The hair alone seemed to unlock a kind of hidden door that Holly never knew existed. Before she knew it, she was hugging her father as if she'd known him all her life.

"My hair's red too," she said.

"Then why are you hiding it behind all that blond stuff?"

"I'll explain later." She hugged her father again.

Shawn doubted that Holly noticed when he stepped out George Foster's back door and went out to the backyard. At least, now, Holly knew that George was a widower and had no other children.

She and her father needed time alone together. He wanted to be alone for a while as well.

He knew what was coming. The thought of never seeing Holly again filled him with a sadness that was worse than death. If Holly had died, he would have been crushed, but he could have moved on. This way, he'd always wonder if there was something more he could have done to save their relationship.

Shawn didn't blame her for not loving him. He just wished that she did. Sometimes he thought she responded to him, but at other times she seemed to push him away.

He never knew what to expect. Still, if she'd ever indicated that he meant more to her than just a good friend, he would have taken her in his arms and never let her go.

He would step back now, let her live her life without him. But he wouldn't stop loving her, ever.

After Holly finished visiting with her father, Shawn would take her out to supper. Then he would drive back to Burbank, and that would be the end of it.

In the living room of the Alameda house, three hours later, Shawn tried to say what had to be said. Somehow, he couldn't.

Finally he just said, "Now that you've found your father, I think I'll drive back to Burbank in the morning. That will give me a few days to rest up before I have to go back to work."

"That's a good idea, Shawn. You deserve a rest after all you've done. And I want you to know how much I appreciate all the help you've given me. I'll never forget it."

I'll never forget *you,* he thought.

And then he left, just like that.

As he was driving off, he heard Holly say, "Drive carefully."

He nodded and waved. He would never see her

again, and she was warning him to drive safely. That had to be the worst ending to a love story in the history of romance.

Holly hadn't given her farewell address after all. When Shawn finally drove away, she collapsed on the green couch and cried her eyes out.

He hadn't seemed upset when she told him good-bye. On the contrary, she thought, he looked relieved.

That night as Holly was taking a shower, her left breast felt different. Her heart palpitated. *No, Lord, say it isn't so.* She was probably imagining things. Holly pressed her fingers in that area of her breast again. She jumped because she felt the lump.

No. I can't have breast cancer, she thought. She was shaking so hard she could barely think. *I need to calm down because this is a huge mistake,* she told herself.

Did breast cancer run in her family? Nobody but Aunt Frances could possibly know. She thought of Suzann and how alike they were in so many ways.

Don't let my sister have cancer, Lord, or me, either.

So much of her life was in turmoil, and in the hands of God. Only time would tell what would come of her reunion with her father or if by some miracle she might yet have a future with Shawn, or whether the lump was malignant. But there was one thing she knew. The Lord heard the prayers of those who accepted His free offer of salvation by Grace and faith in Jesus Christ. Holly intended to pray and expect a miracle.

Chapter Fourteen

Suzann smiled down at the small boy beside her. Robby Sullivan was a sweet child, but her thoughts were elsewhere.

With her hands on her hips, she looked up at the Christmas tree she'd almost finished decorating. The tree stood proudly against the side wall of the church sanctuary between two other Christmas firs.

She'd suggested cedar trees instead. Josh pointed out that many Texas hill country folk were allergic to cedars, especially Mountain cedars. He didn't want the congregation to "tear-up" for any reason other than because they were overcome with emotion as a result of the Christian message they heard at Oak Valley Bible Church.

"Is everything all right, Miss Harmon?" Robby asked, intruding on her recollections.

Suzann blinked, snapping back to the present. "Of course." She gazed down at the child again, noting that he was holding a homemade ornament. "Okay,

Robby, your ornament should add just the right touch. Put it right…there.'' She pointed to an empty limb.

Robby hung the silver ball, grinning smugly.

"That did it,'' Suzann said. "This tree is looking good.''

She'd decked the halls until her fingers were sore, but she had a long way to go before the project was finished. She held her hands out in front of her. Who would have thought Suzann Condry would have two broken fingernails in one day?

"It was nice of you to stay after play practice today, Robby. You're the only one who did. But since I drive you home from practice each afternoon, I don't guess you really had a choice, did you?''

"No, ma'am.''

Suzann smiled. "I do love your honesty.''

Strings of colored lights and child-made ornaments were scattered around the church sanctuary and in every classroom. Suzann thought the decorations gave the inside of the church building a certain glow, signifying the true spirit of Christmas. On second thought, what did Suzann Condry know about the true spirit of Christmas? She wasn't even a Christian.

"Can we go now?'' Robby asked.

"We have three more trees to decorate,'' Suzann said, "and then we're through.''

He cocked his head hesitantly. "But I want to go home, now, so I can watch cartoons on TV.''

"Will you promise not to argue when we stay after play practice tomorrow to finish decorating the church?''

"I—I guess.''

"Robby."

"I mean, yes, Miss Harmon. I won't argue."

Suzann smiled. "That's better."

She'd put her heart into the production of the children's Christmas program. Now a week before the actual performance, Suzann, Josh and the rest of the cast practiced every night as well as immediately after school each day.

After the incident in the choir room, Josh had started driving Suzann home after night services at the church, and this had only drawn them closer. Quick kisses at her door before Suzann went inside became the usual way of saying good-night.

Since Thanksgiving, she and Josh had twice gone on outings with the church youth group to San Antonio, as sponsors. The group planned to go to San Antonio again soon. But would she still be in Oak Valley by then?

Mike had phoned, pressuring her to sign the contract he sent her to make that movie with Steve Norton. Somehow she couldn't. She finally sent back the manuscript, stating that she wasn't interested in making *A Time To Love* after all.

It wasn't entirely because of all the love scenes, either. Suzann was beginning to think she didn't want to make movies anymore. If only she knew what she did want to do in life.

She'd just been standing there, patting the top of Robby's head, while her mind drifted from one thought to another. Robby probably wondered why they weren't getting ready to leave.

"Go get your coat and books, Robby, while I put

away everything else." A lock of his course, reddish hair curled around her forefinger. "Then we can go."

"Thanks, Miss Harmon."

As she watched him race to the classroom where he left his belongings, one thing became clear. She loved working with children, and this little boy had stolen her heart.

After the rehearsal that night, Suzann was putting away some of the props when Josh came into the storage room. Standing on one foot, she stretched in order to return a book to a high shelf.

Josh moved to her side. "Here, let me do that."

His shoulder brushed hers. A feeling of excitement filled Suzann from her head to her toes. She sensed that Josh felt it too.

They turned toward each other. The blue walls behind him paled against the electric glow in his blue eyes.

She felt herself being pulled toward him like a huge magnet. Did Josh sense her feelings for him? Is that why he kept taking their relationship further and further from mere friendship?

His mouth came down on hers. Suzann snuggled closer. His lips moved softly yet firmly over hers. She felt elated, transported.

Suddenly she remembered that Robby had promised to help clean up. She increased the space between them. Robby didn't need to find them together, kissing. She pushed Josh away.

"Hey, what's the matter?" Josh asked.

"Nothing's the matter."

He eyed her inquiringly.

How she'd changed since she moved to Oak Valley. The first time they had kissed, *he'd* pulled away. This time, she did.

"Really," he said, "what's bothering you?"

"Robby Sullivan. He'll be here any moment," she explained. "He said he would help me put things away."

Josh laughed. "If he'd come in a little earlier, he'd have a good reason to say 'Brother Josh has a girl-friend,' wouldn't he?"

"Stop laughing. This isn't funny."

"Yes, it is." He chuckled some more.

"I don't think we should be alone in any room of this church again. Is that clear?"

Josh's grin contained a dash of mischief. "I can agree with that as long as we continue having those 'stolen moments' at the front door of your apartment."

Stolen moments.

Josh would be crushed if he knew about all the stolen moments she'd shared with California types like Greer Fraser—not to mention all the lies she had told Josh since arriving in Oak Valley. Suzann tensed. Someday soon she would have to come clean—to Josh and everybody else in town. She wished she could tell all immediately. If only that were possible.

More and more, recently, she thought about becoming a Christian and what it would mean. But how could she take that step? She was caught in a trap. Until the six months ended, there appeared to be no way out.

* * *

The Christmas program went off perfectly. The Howard brothers made excellent shepherds. Robby Sullivan stole the show as the little drummer boy, and Mrs. Beesley's chocolate cake was the most popular item at the dessert table.

In keeping with their pact, Josh was never alone with Suzann in the church building again. She'd had to find others willing to do the job Josh had been doing. Suzann drafted Robby Sullivan and several other children to help her put the props back in the storeroom after the program that night. Getting the children to actually do it would not be easy.

Suzann was returning a box to an even higher shelf when Dexter Simpson came into the storage room. She knew Dexter attended the Christmas program that night, but she hadn't spoken to him.

"Here, let me do that for you," Dexter said.

Suzann's breath caught. For an instant she thought Josh had spoken those words.

Then Robby started laughing. "Is he your boyfriend too?"

Ignoring the child, Suzann got down from the ladder, then she moved away so the young pastor could take her place. "I'm so glad you were able to come tonight, Brother Simpson."

"I wouldn't have missed it." Dexter shelved the box. "While I'm up here, does anything else go on this shelf?"

"Not a thing."

"That's good." Smiling, he climbed down. "May

I speak to you privately for a minute, Miss Harmon? I have something important to say."

"Of course." She turned toward the children. "All right, kids. Everybody get to work. Just because I'm taking a short break doesn't mean *you* can."

The children moaned loudly.

"No moaning allowed. Now get to work." She looked back at Dexter and smiled. "Now, what is on your mind?"

"After seeing the performance tonight, I'm more convinced than ever that you'd be perfect for that job I mentioned that's coming up at my church in Dallas soon. The job's not filled yet. Is there any way you would reconsider?"

"Really, there isn't. But I appreciate the offer."

"Don't give me a final no," he said. "Think about it until the first of the year. Pray about it," he suggested. "Then give me your answer."

Pray about the unanswered questions on her life? Now, that was something she hadn't tried.

"I wouldn't want to give you false hope," she finally replied. "You see, I know what my answer will be."

"False hope is fine with me. Just don't say no, okay?"

"Okay."

Loud noises distracted her. She turned toward the children just as Robby picked up a broom and started chasing Ben Howard. "Robby Sullivan, put down that broom this instant." Suzann delivered the instructions in a firm tone, yet barely raised her voice.

Robby paused, gazing back at her. "Do I have to?"

"You most certainly do."

"Okay then."

The child put the broom back in the closet where it belonged. Looking slightly embarrassed, he sat down on a large cardboard box, crossing his arms over his chest.

"No need to pout. Just get back to work, Robby."

"Yes, ma'am." Mumbling under his breath, the child got to his feet.

Suzann glanced back at Dexter ashamedly. "Boys will be boys, I guess."

"Yes, and you handled the situation perfectly. Now I'm gladder than ever that you're going to—"

"*Think* about it." She laughed.

"Yes, think about it."

The business owners of Oak Valley planned to keep their stores open until midnight on the following Friday night so everyone could go Christmas shopping. Suzann hadn't decided whether or not she should buy a gift for Josh. But Holly, Kate, and her household staff in California were definitely on her list.

Shortly before they walked out the door on Friday night, Suzann agreed to go Christmas shopping with Kate.

Oak Valley was already lighted and decorated for the holiday season. An entire street was blocked off in the main part of town for the shopping event that night. Gaily lighted trees were everywhere. Christmas music rang out from all directions, and red and green decorations were seen in every store window.

Men dressed up as Santa were featured in several stores. Suzann especially loved the metallic ping of bells when she passed by some of the shops.

A food mall stood off to her left. Farther on, she saw still more booths, highlighting homemade cakes, pies and cookies, as well as toys and other holiday gifts.

A china doll caught her attention, reminding her of one her producer had once sent her from England. She'd been wanting a china doll for a long time and knew they were sold in an area mall.

Back then, she didn't have the freedom to walk down a city street or explore a shopping mall at will. If she trekked through the streets of a California city as she was doing now, a camera would capture her every move, and a director would shout instructions. Only on a movie set could she hope to experience the quaint, old-worldish tone that permeated the celebration that night.

She'd found brotherly love and a sense of community in Oak Valley, Texas. No matter how many expensive sets Hollywood designed or how many savvy actors they signed, Tinsel Town could never duplicate the heart and genuine charm of a small, Texas town like this one.

Kate touched her arm, pointing to a nativity scene off to their right and forcing Suzann back to the present. "I'm so glad to see a manger scene like that here."

"Me too."

"Jesus is the reason for the season," Kate added. "After all, it's His birthday."

"I know."

Suzann gazed at a bookstore that she had noticed when they first arrived. Kate hadn't seemed interested.

"You go on, Kate. I think I'll go in here for a while and see what books they have."

"Are you sure?" Kate asked. "I mean, I know you've hated to be alone since that day when..."

Suzann made a halting gesture. "Stop worrying. I'll be fine."

Suzann entered the store and moved toward the back. A book on twins captured her interest. All at once a flash of light blinked off to her right.

Suzann flinched, blinded. The camera flashed again.

A man with a camera raced outside.

"There he goes," the shop owner said. "Somebody, stop him!"

The man and his camera were gobbled up by the crowd. Suzann wished she'd looked at him more closely. She didn't think she could identify him.

The shop owner hurried over to where Suzann stood. "Why, you're shaking," he said. "Did he hurt you, honey? Or steal something from my store?"

Suzann shook her head. "I wasn't expecting anyone to take my picture, that's all."

"I guess that surprised you, all right. But somebody as young and pretty as you are should be used to being photographed."

"Thanks. But I need to go now."

"What about that book you were looking at? Aren't you going to buy it?"

Suzann was dumbfounded. She'd forgotten she still held the book on twins. Feeling slightly flustered, she handed it to the shop owner. "Maybe I'll buy it some other time. I don't feel much like shopping anymore."

She headed for the door of the shop, then stopped. A cloak of apprehension covered her. It wouldn't be easy to go out again.

Hogwash. She was a grown woman and a worldly one at that. There was no reason to let past experiences destroy her future. She would find Kate, and if she'd finished her shopping, they could leave.

Just then Josh and Kate ambled by, some distance away.

"Wait!" Suzann shouted, waving both her arms.

They just kept walking. She assumed they hadn't seen her. Suzann raced to catch up, but they disappeared, absorbed by the crowd.

Fear mixed with loneliness penetrated the thin coat of boldness she'd manufactured. A mental picture of the man in the green suit filtered through her brain.

Her chest tightened. I can do this, she told herself. She stopped and took in a deep breath of air. Her old sense of determination kicked in then, forcing her to go on.

Suzann presumed Josh and Kate were headed for the parking lot where Kate parked her car. She prayed that she was right and continued in that same direction.

The man with the camera could jump out at any time, but he was probably harmless. It was likely that he was merely an ordinary photojournalist, trying to make a living.

Moreover, she'd been photographed all her life. Why was this any different?

But everything was different since she'd come to Oak Valley. She wasn't ready yet to give up her life as Holly. Or to give up Josh.

She wanted to feel Josh's hand laced with hers— to feel his arm around her. But that was unrealistic. He wouldn't always be there for her. Nobody would. It was time to get used to it.

In days—hours, the entire story could come out in the tabloids. She imagined the headlines. "Suzann Condry Switches Identities with Twin Sister." At least those headlines would tell the truth for a change.

She searched the crowd again, looking for Kate and Josh as she headed for the parking lot. She turned a corner and saw the parking lot straight ahead. Kate and Josh stood by Kate's car. But why did they look so sad?

Suzann rushed over to them.

"We need to get to the hospital right away." Josh's throaty voice indicated that he'd been crying. "Robby Sullivan was in— Robby was in an accident a little while ago, and he isn't expected— He isn't doing well at all."

Suzann felt her body turn to stone. *No, not Robby*, she prayed. A silent cry burned through her. This couldn't be happening. Not to sweet little Robby.

Dazed by the news, Suzann didn't realize they had reached the hospital until Josh opened the door on her side. As she got out, she was still too stunned to hear much of what was being said.

"He's in ICU," Josh said as they rushed inside. "Of course, only the family are allowed to see him."

A crowd from the church had gathered at the ICU waiting room. Nobody seemed to know anything about Robby's condition.

"Let's pray," somebody said.

Suzann nodded. Without a second thought, she joined the circle of prayer warriors, standing in the middle of the room. With Josh on her right side and Kate on her left, Suzann bowed her head and closed her eyes.

Josh's hand felt warm and moist. Hers were damp too, but it didn't matter. Nothing would matter until Robby was well and happy again.

Josh led the prayer. Suzann was praying so hard on her own that she scarcely heard him. She'd prayed many times since she came to Oak Valley but never with such a sense of purpose.

She thought of her own life—of how unworthy she was to ask the Lord for anything. But she intended to pray anyway because she had to.

Josh squeezed her hand. "Amen." Then he led her to a chair near the door.

Kate went over and sat down by Mrs. Beesley.

"I know how you feel," Josh said tenderly, "because all of us here feel exactly the same way."

"Does anyone really know what happened?" Suzann asked.

"Not the details." Josh brushed back a lock of hair that had fallen across her face. "We just know that

Robby was crossing the street in front of his house when he was hit by a car.''

"Don't tell me he was hit by a drunk driver."

"No, a teenage driver." He cleared his throat. "We think he was hit by his older sister, Marge."

She gasped. "How awful." Suzann looked down, covering her mouth with her right hand to hold in a sob. "Marge must be devastated."

"She is."

Suzann lifted her head. "You've talked to her?"

"When they were loading Robby into the ambulance. Later, we just prayed."

She wanted to pray again too. But did God hear the prayers of someone like Suzann Condry? After a moment, she looked around the room.

"Where's the family?" Suzann asked. "I need to tell them how sorry I am."

"I guess Robby's parents are still inside with him. Marge and the rest of the family are back at the house with Pastor Jones."

Suzann bit her lower lip. Memories of Robby Sullivan appeared before her. Under all that boyish charm, Robby had such a lust for life and such a sweet nature. She recalled the freckles that covered his upturned nose and those expressive green eyes. She winced, remembering the times she'd had to scold him. Once she'd even made him cry.

"I wish I hadn't yelled at Robby the day before the Christmas program."

Josh took both her hands in his and squeezed them. "Don't think about that now. You know how Robby adores you. Why, he was the one who kept insisting I get you as my assistant youth director.''

Suzann smiled through her tears. "He was?"

Josh blinked, then nodded.

"Oh, Josh, he just can't die." She swallowed to keep from crying. "He won't, will he?"

"No matter what happens, just remember that God loves Robby even more than we do. And keep praying."

"I will."

A gray-haired nurse came out of ICU. Everybody stood as if they had been told to do so. Josh stepped forward.

"I'm Josh Gallagher, the assistant pastor. Is there anything new you can tell us?"

"There's been no change," the nurse said, "but I do have a message from the child's parents. It seems that there are a lot of other people waiting outside. They can't all get into the waiting room here, because there isn't room."

"And the message?" Josh said.

"Oh, yes. The family requested that everybody go to the church and hold a prayer service tonight for Robby. Mr. and Mrs. Sullivan said that would do more good than waiting out here."

"Please tell them I'll get to that right away."

Suzann had admired Josh from the moment she first saw him, but never more than when he organized the prayer group at the church that night. In minutes he'd phoned the local radio station, asking them to announce the prayer meeting on their station. Then he phoned several TV and radio stations in San Antonio, requesting that they do the same.

People started pouring into the church sanctuary long before Suzann and Josh arrived. Suzann had attended many church services and prayer meetings since coming to Oak Valley. But the service for Robby Sullivan was the most moving.

Pastor Jones conducted the service. She'd expected Josh to sit up front with the pastor. However, he sat in the pew right beside her, holding her hand the whole time. If the congregation didn't know Suzann was Josh's girlfriend before, they knew it now.

She wanted to go back to the hospital after the service, but Josh talked her out of it.

"It's late," he said, "and you look tired. Besides, there's really nothing more we can do."

Then he drove her home.

Suzann couldn't sleep. Two hours later, she drove to the hospital again to see Robby. Until she reached the door of the hospital, she hadn't even realized that it was the first time she'd driven at night since she was alone in the church choir room. She'd just jumped in her car and roared off. Her love for Robby proved stronger than her fears. A sense of awe encircled her.

The hospital was closed. She had known it would be.

I need to get in there, Lord, to pray. Please find a way.

A nurse in a white uniform went in through a side door of the hospital. Suzann hadn't noticed that door when they went in earlier. When the nurse disappeared down a hall, Suzann slipped inside. Pretending she belonged there would not be a problem for an actress.

She went straight to the ICU to see if there was any news. Robby's aunt assured her there wasn't. Suzann had a deep desire to pray again. And what better place than the chapel right there at the hospital?

The chapel was small and dimly lighted. A huge, open Bible on a stand centered the front of the room. A wooden cross towered behind it. She hadn't expected to see Josh here, but guessed that he'd been allowed to stay with Robby since he was a clergyman and close to the family.

Josh sat in a pew near the front. She settled into a pew near the back. He hadn't seen her yet, and she was glad. She had some serious praying to do and didn't want to be interrupted.

Heavenly Father, I have no right to ask You for anything. But, please, heal little Robby Sullivan. His family loves him so much, and so does everybody else here in Oak Valley, including me.

And Lord, Josh said that You know everything. If that's true, You know I've been thinking of becoming a Christian. But I really need proof that You're who You say You are. Show me that You're real, Lord, and I'll follow You forever. Amen.

Chapter Fifteen

Suzann lifted her head. Josh had left the chapel. Surely he had seen her on his way out.

She went back to the ICU waiting room. Josh sat on a couch, praying. A white handkerchief was wadded between his folded hands.

Paralyzed with alarm, Suzann stopped. Did this mean Robby was—? She hesitated to even think the word *dead,* much less say it. Invisible fingernails tore her heart.

Tears strained to be released. She craved to be comforted, yearned to feel Josh's arms around her, to hear gentle words of sympathy and love.

Josh looked up then. A smile shone through. "I have good news."

"Good news? Oh, Josh." Suzann flew into his arms, burying her face in his shoulder. He held her so close that she heard the tender beating of his heart.

"The doctors say that Robby will completely recover."

"Praise God."

"Amen." He nodded in agreement. "Except for a few minor scrapes and bruises, Robby will be as good as new."

"That's wonderful."

"Yes, it is." His calming grin reassured her. "The doctors say he came through against all odds."

"What do *you* think?"

"I think we know what *really* happened because we know who healed that boy."

"Yes." She'd asked for a sign from God, and He had given her one. *Thank you, Lord.*

"I'd prayed," Josh said, "that Robby's healing would be used as a witness to others. That many would be saved because they knew Robby was dying, and God cured him."

Suzann wanted to tell Josh that she was on the brink of making the most important decision that she would ever make. Yet an unseen obstruction blocked her throat, making it impossible to share her good news with anyone.

Josh merely stood there, holding her. He would have no way of knowing the struggle going on inside her. She longed to tell Josh that his prayer was about to be answered, that she was about to come to Jesus—partly because of Robby Sullivan's miracle.

Suzann closed her eyes. Unknown to Josh, she prayed the sinner's prayer, inviting Jesus into her heart and life.

Joy unspeakable filled every part of her. If only she could tell Josh about the excitement she felt. He thought she was already saved. Knowing that, how could she explain what had just occurred?

Pastor Jones always said that the moment a sinner was saved, the angels in Heaven rejoiced. Suzann pondered whether heavenly angels might at that moment be having a party in her honor. It pleased her to think that they were.

As a Christian, she would look to the Lord for answers now. But with one reservation. She couldn't tell Josh or the congregation at Oak Valley Bible Church who she really was until she figured out the best way to do it.

Baptism was something she would need to consider. But how? When? She could imagine the controversy she would cause if she waltzed up to the front of the church some Sunday morning, requesting baptism. Why Sister Winslow and Mrs. Beesley were likely to fall right out of their pews.

Though glorious in all ways, her salvation was not without its own set of problems. Josh would know her true identity now, and that might well be the deathblow to their make-believe romance.

She swallowed to keep from spilling tears all over the front of his blue-and-white flannel shirt. How could she be so happy about her salvation and Robby's recovery, and at the same time feel so disappointed at the thought of losing Josh?

Suzann shut her eyes and prayed again.

Holly was frantic when she left the doctor's office on Monday afternoon. Her doctor had confirmed her worst nightmare: he was as worried about the lump in her breast as Holly was. Since then, she had paced the floor, considering who she should tell about her upcoming biopsy.

She finally resolved not to tell Suzann. Her sister was in the middle of some kind of crisis. Though Holly didn't know the nature of Suzann's problem, she knew it was serious.

Holly decided not to tell anyone except her parents back in Texas about her future hospital stay. She also planned to request that they not say anything about it to Shawn.

She phoned her sister the morning after Suzann's conversion, intending to request prayer for an anonymous woman in Alameda who might have breast cancer. However, before Holly could say any of the things she'd planned to say, Suzann started talking about Jesus.

Bursting with gladness and enthusiasm, Suzann related that on the previous night she had accepted Jesus and was now a born-again Christian, partly as the result of a miracle. Then Suzann told Holly about Robby's healing. Both sisters wept with joy.

"Before my conversion experience," Suzann said, "I never realized how happy I would be just knowing I was saved and forgiven of all my sins. You see, I was spiritually blind. But now I can see, Holly, I really can—just like it says in that song, 'Amazing Grace.'"

"I believe you," Holly said. "This is so great, and an answer to my prayers."

Holly hated to spoil her sister's good news by discussing her prayer request. Still, she would be going into the hospital the next morning for a biopsy. She wanted to know people were praying for her.

During a lull in their telephone conversation, Holly explained that she had a friend with a lump in her breast who needed prayer. Suzann assured her that she would put Holly's friend on the prayer list at Oak Valley Bible Church. Soon after that, the dialogue ended.

Holly checked into the hospital the next morning, feeling lonely and afraid. She missed Shawn desperately, wished he would be at her side, before, during and after the operation. But she wouldn't phone him. That part of her life was over.

Holly pulled the heavy blue, terry-cloth robe from her suitcase, slipping it on over her pale blue, silk nightgown. Nobody would accuse her of being a movie star in this outfit, she thought, eyeing her image with amusement.

Shawn McDowell had changed her in unexpected ways. Now she didn't automatically squelch the laughter that often welled up inside her over ordinary things like her favorite blue robe. More Christians should be like Shawn. They should be full of the joy of the Lord in all circumstances.

Her family were flying in from El Paso that night. She wondered if they would notice the change in her. Holly took comfort in knowing her parents and her two younger brothers would be waiting when she came out of surgery, and tried not to think about Shawn and Suzann. From now on, she was going to

dwell on the light side of life. Shawn had taught her
that a merry heart really was like a medicine.

The *swish* of footfalls on the brown carpet alerted
her. Holly turned toward the sound and found Shawn
at the foot of her hospital bed. Without thinking, she
reached for him.

"You can run, but you can't hide forever." Shawn
came around the side of her bed and embraced her
fervently. "You should have known I'd track you
down sooner or later."

"It's so good to see you, and I'm glad it was
sooner."

"Me too. And I like the glasses and auburn hair.
Now you really do look like a female Clark Kent."

"If I take off my glasses will I turn into Super
Girl?"

"There's one way to find out." He reached out,
plucked the glasses off her nose, and dropped a quick
kiss on her lips. He reached for both her hands and
held them. "Holly, there's something I—"

"How'd you find out where I was? Are you claim-
ing super powers too?"

"Only when someone I care about is involved."
He gave her a look so full of meaning that Holly was
afraid to let herself absorb it. "I called your parents,
and they told me where you were."

"Does Suzann know?"

"I'm not sure." He dropped a kiss on her forehead.
"I know your parents tried calling her yesterday and
last night. But she didn't answer."

"So, how are you doing?" he asked.

"I'm making it." Holly's lower lip quivered. "I

know what a wonderful Christian you are, Shawn. Would you mind if we prayed?''

''That's one of the reasons I'm here.''

What are the other reasons? she wanted to ask.

She was glad she hadn't asked that question aloud. She feared she wasn't ready to hear his reasons. What if they weren't the ones she longed to hear?

Still holding her hands, Shawn bowed his head, closed his eyes, and spoke to God in a heartfelt way. Holly knew the Lord heard. Tears stung her eyelids.

When they finished praying, he said, ''Holly, I have something to ask you.'' He reached inside his jacket for something.

Holly was elated that Shawn had come. She'd prayed that he would. But she wasn't ready for more than a visit. Not until she was released from the hospital with a clean bill of health, she told herself. She wanted Shawn's love, not his pity. Determined not to give in to tears again, Holly sought to lighten the situation, as Shawn had always done for her during tense moments.

Glancing at her untouched lunch tray, she frowned. ''Do you like peas and carrots?'' she asked.

He laughed. ''Sometimes.'' He appeared both amused and puzzled by her question. He removed his hand from inside his jacket, empty. ''It depends on how they are prepared. Why?''

''I need a good friend who would be willing to eat my peas and carrots for me.'' Holly fought off the urge to beg Shawn to go ahead with whatever he was about to say. Instead, she smiled cheerfully. ''Are you that friend?''

"You want me to eat peas and carrots?" he asked. "Now?"

"Now. You see, my nurse won't like it one bit if she comes back in here and finds out I didn't eat all my lunch."

He grinned. "This is crazy." He picked up the extra fork from her tray. "Still, I think you just got yourself a vegetable-eating friend." Jokingly, he held his nose. "That is, if I can manage to swallow this stuff."

Holly laughed. She was doing the right thing. She knew it. She loved Shawn too much to let him propose until they both knew more about her future health status.

He stuck the fork in the peas. "And after I finish eating this mess, and those doctors are through running their tests, I have a package I'd like you to open. Deal?"

Holly's heart bounded. She'd waited a long time to hear what she hoped Shawn was about to say to her. Surely, she could wait another twenty-four hours.

"On second thought," Shawn said, dropping the fork back on the plate. "There's no time like the present." He hesitated. "I love you, Holly. That's all I'm going to say for now."

Holly stared at him, unable to move or speak. I love you too, Shawn, she wanted to say. In spite of all her reasons for holding in her feelings, joy flooded her heart, crowding out all else. She trembled with the force of it. "I love you too, Shawn."

His gaze grew tender. A smile slowly emerged. "I would have told you sooner," he said, "but sometimes you pull away from me.'' Shawn took her in his arms and held her close. ''I was afraid you wouldn't return my love. It's an answer to a prayer to learn that you care for me, too.''

Holly cleared her throat. ''Shawn?''

''Yes, darling.''

''Could I—could I have a look at that package now?''

''I thought you'd never ask.''

Suzann had learned to love and trust God and others in Oak Valley, Texas. She'd also fallen in love with a wonderful man. The Lord seemed to be encouraging her to do two things—tell the congregation at Oak Valley Bible Church that she was a Christian, and tell them who she really was.

She'd told Dexter she would think about the job he offered her, and she found herself considering it seriously. Suzann knew she wanted a teaching ministry.

But after Dexter learned the truth about her past, he might not want her for the job at his church. Maybe she'd fly up to Dallas anyway and find out for sure. And if not Dallas…?

She would worry about that when and if the time came.

When the altar call was given at church on Christmas Eve morning, Suzann went forward. A hush fell on the congregation.

Miss Harmon was already supposed to be saved. Pastor Jones stood at the front of the church, waiting for Suzann to make her way down from the choir.

Every eye was on her. The preacher probably thought she wanted prayer or planned to rededicate her life. If he only knew.

Snow-white eyebrows accented the minister's pale blue eyes and silver hair. He leaned toward her, waiting to hear her request.

"I've accepted Jesus," Suzann whispered.

His heavy brows lifted. An expression of astonishment appeared on his kind, fatherly face. "Just?" he mouthed.

"Yes."

A gentle light glimmered in his blue eyes. "So what do you want to do now?"

"I'm requesting baptism," she said.

The pastor held both her hands in his, and he prayed with her.

When he finished, Suzann opened her mouth to tell him her true identity. No words came.

She felt incomplete, somehow. Something else needed to be done, and she wasn't doing it. She should tell the preacher who she really was, but she simply couldn't—not now. A feeling of foreboding crept over her.

After the service, Suzann stood at the front of the church to shake hands with a long line of church members. She'd spoken briefly with Mrs. Beesley, when someone else sidled in beside her. Suzann turned, and Kate hugged her.

"It's a pleasure," Kate said, "to finally meet the church librarian."

Had Kate discerned all along that she wasn't Holly?

Before Suzann had time to give it much thought, Josh squeezed her hand. Confusion gleamed in his eyes. He had questions that demanded answers. She intended to respond, but not now.

After Josh moved on, Suzann noticed that the man who had been following her and taking pictures was also in the welcome line. Her chest contracted. She hadn't thought that she would recognize him, but she did. He's going to make a scene, she thought.

The photojournalist shook her hand. "Glad to see you, Miss Condry," he whispered. "You'll be reading more about yourself in an upcoming issue of our tabloid newspaper. And thanks for joining the church this morning. That will mean still another scoop for my newspaper."

She forced herself to relax, smiling at the Howard brothers who were next in line. She'd always known the guy with the camera would catch up with her, eventually. However, she hadn't expected it to happen at the church.

Suddenly she knew what the Lord wanted her to do.

Before leaving that Sunday morning, Suzann told Pastor Jones that she wanted to give her testimony at church that night.

Holly had waited until almost one p.m. to make her telephone call. She knew Suzann would be attending church that morning, and she wanted to catch her before she left the apartment again.

The small incision in Holly's left breast ached slightly. She fingered the heavy bandage under her blue silk nightgown. Turning on her right side, she switched the receiver to her other ear. *Ring, ring.*

"Hello."

"Oh, Suzann, there you are."

Holly had counted on sharing all the recent developments in her life. However, Suzann took over the conversation again, exclaiming that she'd requested baptism in church that morning and intended to give her testimony that night.

Holly was delighted. It was what she'd been praying for all along. But before Holly could say so much as "Praise the Lord," Suzann was explaining her true feelings for Josh Gallagher.

Holly decided that if she got to tell her sister anything at all, she would lead with something upbeat and positive.

"Shawn and I found our real father, Suzann," Holly said at last. "And I can't wait for you to meet him. I also met our aunt, our mother's only sister."

"You met George Foster?"

"I sure did."

"Why, that's great news. What about our mother?"

Holly wondered how to begin. "Our mother died…a long time ago."

"No!"

"I'm afraid it's true, Suzann. I'm so sorry."

Suzann didn't say anything for a moment or two. "I—I wish she was still alive."

"Me too," Holly said. "But did I mention that she was a Christian? I couldn't be happier about that."

"Oh, I'm glad too," Suzann said, "and please tell

George Foster and our aunt that I can't wait to meet them.''

"I already have, because I knew you'd want me to."

Holly paused before continuing. Suzann still didn't know about her surgery, and Holly still wasn't sure how to tell her.

A warning light came on inside Holly's brain. Why had she not told her sister the truth? She had lied by omission.

Please forgive me, Lord, for lying. I'm truly sorry.

"I've had some surgery, Suzann. The doctors found a lump in my breast. Forgive me for not telling you earlier."

Suzann's heavy gasp cut all the way to the center of Holly's being. "Why didn't you tell me? I would have flown out there to be with you."

"I should have told you. Christians should never tell lies, even little white ones."

"And you're sure you're all—all right?" Suzann asked. "There's no cancer?"

"None whatsoever. I couldn't be better."

Holly's stomach tightened. She knew she'd disappointed her sister.

"New Christians like you," Holly began, "tend to think that older Christians, like me, never make mistakes. But we do—all the time."

"You mean Christians sin?"

"Nobody but Jesus is perfect, Suzann. Of course I mess up and sin once in a while, even though I try not to. My feet get dirty walking around in a flawed world, but Jesus is kind and washes my feet for me."

"Then if Christians still sin, how is that any different from the way I was before I got saved?"

"The difference," Holly said, "is that now the Lord lives inside your heart. He will remind you to repent, immediately, when you sin or make mistakes. And as soon as you repent, you're washed clean again."

This was a lot to swallow at one sitting. Perhaps it was time for Holly to add a pinch of humor to the stew. Her diamond engagement ring caught the light coming in from the window of her hospital room.

"Guess what I'm doing?" Holly said.

"I can't imagine."

"I'm looking at my engagement ring."

"You're *engaged?*"

"You better believe I am. Shawn McDowell asked me to marry him as soon as I returned from surgery this morning, and I said yes before he changed his mind."

Shawn walked into her room, then, carrying a handful of red roses. The flowers' fragrant aroma contrasted with the heavier scent of rubbing alcohol.

"Hold on a minute, Suzann. I want to give my new fiancé a big kiss hello."

"I like that idea," Shawn said.

Holly put the receiver on the bed beside her, and reached for Shawn with both arms. She knew she'd never tire of his kisses—not for at least the next sixty or seventy years. Perhaps longer.

Somehow the receiver had slipped to the edge of the bed. If she didn't do something, it would end up on the floor.

"Excuse me, Shawn." Holly grabbed the receiver.

"Tell Suzann that her future brother-in-law is dying to meet her," said Shawn.

"Shawn said—"

"I heard." Suzann giggled. "And tell Shawn that I'm looking forward to meeting him too."

"Shawn and I are getting married on Valentine's Day, and we want you to be my maid of honor. Will you, Suzann? Please say yes."

"Yes, I'd love to."

"You'll need to wear a pink dress," Holly said. "But I saw plenty of dresses that should do nicely in those huge walk-in closets of yours."

Holly was happy that all *her* prayers had been answered. Yet she couldn't help wishing that all the walls standing between Suzann and Josh would tumble down immediately.

Suzann put on her late mother's heart-shaped locket and drove to the church that night to give her testimony. There was no reason not to wear the locket now. Everyone would know her identity soon enough.

After she went forward and accepted Jesus that morning, the congregation at Oak Valley Bible Church appeared to pay special attention to Suzann as she stepped down from the choir area at the front of the sanctuary and approached the podium.

Butterflies swarmed inside her stomach. She wiped her damp brow with the back of her hand.

Facing the crowd, she tried to smile. "Merry Christmas." She gripped the sides of the wooden podium with trembling fingers. Out of the corner of her eye, she saw Josh smile as if to encourage her.

Would Josh still be smiling after he heard her testimony?

She should have told him what was in her testimony before she presented it to the entire congregation. Josh deserved to be informed. She could only pray that somehow he would understand.

If she'd known how to relate her story, she would have divulged everything earlier. Were it not for the Lord's urging, she wouldn't be standing on this podium even now.

She cleared her throat and took a deep breath.

The photojournalist—the same man she had talked to that morning—sat in the first row. The cameraman's smile was anything but supportive.

"My name is *not* Holly Harmon," she said.

She saw shocked expressions throughout the auditorium, mouths gaping open in disbelief. She prayed quickly for Divine help.

"My name is Suzann Condry, and I'm Holly Harmon's identical twin sister. I came to Oak Valley, pretending to be my sister, so that I could get away from the life I led in Hollywood."

Josh looked flabbergasted.

"I never expected to find Jesus along the way." She waited before going on to let her words sink in. "I know you have questions, and in time I intend to answer all of them. First of all, Holly's alive and well, and she's living in my home in California. And she's impatient to come back to Oak Valley and see all of you again. I hope to find a teaching ministry some-where.''

She paused again. This time, however, she con-sciously avoided eye contact with Josh. ''No, I won't be going back to Hollywood, and I'll never make movies again. That part of my life is gone forever. I'm a new person, born again by the Spirit of God. The person I once was is no more.''

She described in detail how God had changed her life, ending her testimony by asking the congregation to forgive her. When she finished speaking, she headed straight for the exit at the side of the auditorium—not looking to her left or to her right lest she see expressions of condemnation.

Though sad at the thought of leaving Josh and her other friends in Oak Valley, she'd never felt such peace in her entire life.

She headed for the church library, to retrieve the handbag that she'd left at her desk. Josh suddenly appeared beside her. He took her by the hand and led her to a quiet corner behind a bookcase.

''I've accepted the call to become a pastor over in Blessed Hope,'' he said. ''And when I start my min-istry there I could sure use a wife who sings hymns beautifully and is great with children.'' He kissed her then, wiping away all her doubts. ''Want the job?''

He wants to *marry* me, she thought. Even after all those things I said publicly in my testimony!

''I'm in love with you, Suzann.''

Suzann. He called me Suzann, she thought.

''I want you to promise to marry me,'' he said,

"and you're spending Christmas Day with my family if I have to tie you to the back of my truck."

Her heart leapt with joy. "Yes."

"Yes, you'll marry me? Or yes, you'll eat Christmas dinner with my folks?"

"Yes to both. Yes, yes, yes."

As Josh reached down to kiss her again, a loud round of applause rang out from somewhere behind them. Until that instant, she hadn't realized that some of the people from Oak Valley Bible Church had followed them to the church library.

Then Robby Sullivan said, "I knew all along that Brother Josh was sweet on the church librarian."

Everybody laughed.

"When's the wedding?" Mrs. Beesley asked.

"As soon as possible." Josh draped his arm possessively around Suzann's shoulders. "I don't want this lady to get away."

"Not a chance," Suzann put in. "And my twin sister, Holly, is getting married on Valentine's Day. I think I'd like to make it a double wedding. What do you think?"

Josh winked at Suzann. "I think that's a great idea."

Suzann silently thanked God for answering all her prayers. Then she gazed back at the man she loved.

"I'm yours, Josh," she said tenderly, "now and forever after."

Epilogue

A scattering of white, pink and red flowers filled the sanctuary of Oak Valley Bible Church, contrasting with the ivory-colored walls and dark oak pews. The air was scented with roses. The congregation was gathered on Valentine's Day to witness a double wedding.

Suzann gripped her bouquet of pink roses to keep her hands from shaking. But peace and serenity had fallen on her earlier when she and her sister had stood side by side in the church sanctuary in identical, antique-white, Victorian wedding gowns, singing "Amazing Grace" together as a duet for the first time. Yet nothing compared to the excitement and happiness she felt now, breathlessly standing with Josh before the altar to speak their wedding vows.

Josh clasped her hand, smiling with that special grin of his. On her other side, Holly stood beside Shawn. Suzann rejoiced anew.

Suzann handed the bouquet to Kate. Then she

laughed to herself as Kate, in a deep pink maid of honor's dress, struggled to hold two bridal bouquets, plus her garland of pink flowers, at the same time. Suzann was afraid Kate might drop them—until she saw that determined look on her friend's face. Kate was going to make a fantastic lawyer. Suzann was glad they talked things out and Kate held no grudges for her deception, or for winning Josh.

Suzann turned slightly, smiling over her shoulder at her birth father, George Foster. Did her white veil hide her face? Or did he know she was thinking of him and her maternal aunt at that very instant?

At last, her gaze shifted to Pastor Jones's strong, compassionate face. Love filled her heart, and a holy joy sent her spirit soaring.

Suzann turned back to her future husband, smiled, and sent up a heartfelt prayer. *Thank you, Lord, for Josh, and for Holly and Shawn, and for answering all my prayers. And thank you, Lord, for Grace— Amazing Grace—that saved a sinner like me.*

It had been hazy and cold outside since the day after Christmas, and the weatherman had predicted thunder showers.

Then suddenly, there was a break in the clouds. Sunshine streamed through the stained-glass windows like a heavenly spotlight, illuminating the two happy couples as they said their wedding vows.

Suzann and Holly shared a brief but knowing glance, and a silent prayer for one another, thanking the Lord for the true love they'd each found and asking for His blessings on their married life from this day forward.

* * * * *

Dear Reader,

As a child, I was a poor speller and was in the lowest of four reading groups. Some might have written me off as doomed to failure. Yet two fourth-grade teachers in Kingsville, Texas, not only thought I was talented in singing and creative writing, they shared those thoughts with me. I call those life-changing words of encouragement *Blessings,* and it is not coincidental that my novel is titled *Brides and Blessings.*

The Bible talks a lot about blessings. Christians are told not only to bless one another with good things but to bless the Lord, as well—*Psalms* 103:1-2. If I could say one thing to parents and teachers today, it would be to look for the good in children and bless them by telling them they have worth.

It worked for me.

Love and Blessings to All,

Molly Bull

Continuing in February 1999 from Love Inspired®...

SUDDENLY!

Celebrate the joy of unexpected parenthood in this heartwarming series about some very unexpected special deliveries.

SUDDENLY DADDY (June 1998)
SUDDENLY MOMMY (August 1998)

Don't miss the last book in the series...

SUDDENLY MARRIED
by Loree Lough

Noah vowed to keep religion in his children's lives even though he was struggling with his own faith. Then he met Sunday school teacher Dara Mackenzie, who taught his children about their religion, and taught Noah about the healing power of prayer, faith and love.

Don't miss SUDDENLY MARRIED in February 1999 from

Available at your favorite retail outlet.

ILISM